THE OUTLANDS DEMON

OTHER BOOKS BY ANNA DURAND

THE OUTLANDS DEMON

The Devil's Outlands, Book Two

ANNA DURAND

JACOBSVILLE BOOKS · MARIETTA, OHIO

THE OUTLANDS DEMON

ISBN: 978-1-958144-44-2 (paperback)
ISBN: 978-1-958144-45-9 (ebook)
ISBN:978-1-958144-46-6 (audiobook)

Jacobsville Books
www.JacobsvilleBooks.com

Publisher's Cataloging-in-Publication Data
provided by Five Rainbows Cataloging Services

Names: Durand, Anna.
Title: The outlands demon / Anna Durand.
Description: Marietta, OH : Jacobsville Books, 2024.
Identifiers: ISBN 978-1-958144-44-2 (paperback) | ISBN 978-1-958144-45-9 (ebook) | ISBN 978-1-958144-46-6 (audiobook)
Subjects: LCSH: Man-woman relationships--Fiction. | Magic--Fiction. | Time travel--Fiction. | Paranormal romance stories. | Romance fiction. | BISAC: FICTION / Romance / Paranormal /General. | FICTION / Romance / Fantasy. | FICTION / Romance / Suspense. | GSAFD: Romantic suspense fiction. | Occult fiction. | Love stories.
Classification: LCC PS3604.U724 O97 2024 (print) | LCC PS3604.U724 (ebook) | DDC 813/.6--dc23.

CHAPTER ONE

Zaen'imuth

WHEN A GREAT INJUSTICE HAS BEEN DONE, SOMEONE MUST PAY FOR IT, no matter the cost. Every demon knows this to be true. I might have despised my father, but I cannot allow his murder to go unavenged. When the killer is a mortal, however, the injustice becomes even more profound, and therefore the redress must be of equal magnitude. I am the crown prince of the underworld, after all—or I should have been, if another demon hadn't stolen the throne from me.

The human female who destroyed my father must die an excruciating death.

Yet how can I avenge myself when I languish in a prison cell?

The walls around me pulsate with ribbons of smoldering crimson. Walls of blood. To remind me of my fate. Eventually, Rahn'omith will torture and kill me, just as I need to torture and kill the mortal woman who slaughtered my father. The cycle of death and fury never ends.

Perhaps it should. But the very idea is unthinkable for most demons.

The crimson walls of my cell abruptly stop pulsating. The doorway telescopes open, and a warrior from

Rahn'omith's clan marches inside to seize my arm and drag me away. He doesn't speak or even glance at me. As we walk into the cavernous throne room, I count at least a hundred individuals gathered here to watch the spectacle that we all know Rahn'omith will engage in to prove he is the king. Any demon who needs to prove his might and power to his underlings is no leader. And one who must imprison his rival is a weakling.

My guard halts us at the base of the throne dais, no doubt to make the usurper king seem larger. He sits twelve steps above the rest of us. I remain shackled, as I have been for the duration of my imprisonment. The guard disappears into the crowd.

I hold my head high, glaring at Rahn'omith.

He sits there with his hands on the throne's arms, tapping his fingers. "Don't you wonder why I've summoned you?"

The usurper king begins with a question, a sign of weakness. My father, despite his many faults, would never have behaved this way. He would be shouting at me, not asking what I think.

I ignore the question and narrow my gaze on the usurper.

Rahn'omith slams his fists down on his throne. "Answer me, Zaen'imuth!"

I shrug one shoulder. "Your question doesn't interest me."

He leaps off the throne, marching down the steps to stand before me. "I've summoned you here so that I may mete out your final punishment."

Though I exhale a long sigh, I give him no other response.

Rahn'omith slants toward me, and spittle sprays from his lips as he shouts at me. "I could have killed you immediately after your father's death. But I spared you. Bow down before me and express your eternal gratitude."

"Never."

"You wish to die, then?"

I chuckle. "Full of questions, aren't you? Only a weak ruler asks anything of his subjects. A true king commands his people."

"You are the last one who should call me weak. Your own father hacked the horns off your head. Might as well have castrated you."

"But I can still fuck women, with or without horns." I smirk. "Just ask your wife. I pleasured her many times before you became king. After my imprisonment, she often sneaked into my cell to get her fix. The queen of the underworld can't get enough of me."

Rahn'omith shakes his fists and roars.

I go on smirking.

"Your lies are the final nail in your coffin," the false king declares. "I hereby strip you of your military rank. No longer will you serve as general of the collective armies of the demon hordes."

"What a crushing blow to my ego. Leading an army of depraved, slavering monsters was my lifelong dream. Most of them can't even speak, but I appreciate a challenge."

My sarcasm seems to fly right past his head. "Then I will take great pleasure in removing you from your station." He saunters up the steps and surveys the crowd, then waves his arms in a melodramatic gesture. "I hereby pronounce that Zaen'imuth has been stripped of his rank and dishonorably discharged from the collective armies. I have other plans for him."

I maintain my disinterested expression, only in part to annoy him. His use of the term dishonorably discharged sounds like a joke. Since when do demons have honor? He must have spent too much time in the mortal world and picked up the military phrase there.

Rahn'omith throws his arms up. "Zaen'imuth shall be executed immediately!"

Of course he wants to turn my execution into a spectacle, but I've had enough of this nonsense. After months in solitary confinement, I have finally discovered an opening that will let me escape—thanks to the false king's arrogance. He always assumes too much.

I tap into my powers, and the shackles crumble away. "Everything that should have been mine will belong to me once again. Watch your back, usurper. I won't forget what you've done."

Just as he flings himself through the air, aiming for me, I vanish.

Since I have no time to target my landing point, I wind up spiraling through the aether, zapped by the magical energies that roil within the empty space. At last, I crash down onto bare, cold earth. My face is mashed into the dirt. Seconds elapse while I struggle to recover from the bone-crunching power of my arrival in whatever place this is. Not the demon world. I would recognize the odors of that domain. But I can smell something earthy and fresh.

Definitely not the underworld.

Fortunately, the usurper's wife had sneaked into my cell last night. Her lust for me had generated enough magics to give me the boost I needed to escape. That surge has faded now.

I push myself up into a kneeling position, brushing off the dirt, and scan the vicinity. A pale moon hangs in the sky. A soft breeze rustles my hair. The scent of...things I've never smelled before surrounds me. In the distance, a creature howls. Is that a wolf? We don't have those in the underworld, but I know they do exist. I can't tell if it's a normal wolf or the supernatural kind. I've heard that mundane wolves do exist in the mortal world. Having rarely visited that domain, I know almost nothing about it. My father forbade me to go there unless he accompanied me.

I rise to my feet and allow my demon senses to guide me. As I amble down the deserted dirt path, I begin to see large, rectangular objects up ahead. The closer I come to those shapes, the more details I discern. I believe those are buildings. I vaguely recall seeing them during one of those trips with my father, when I was much younger. Once, a demoness told me of a place called the Outlands. Only later did I learn that my father ruled over that supernatural realm, which lies somewhere between the underworld and the human world.

My father never shared anything with me, not even tales of his battles.

While I continue down the dirt path toward the buildings, I begin to perceive more details. Demon vision is much better than that of any human. Still, my eyes needed time to adjust to the darkness and the strange new environment. Now I see everything.

I halt in the middle of the dirt path, turning in a circle to take in my surroundings. I believe this is a "street" or perhaps a "road." I've heard both terms. The settlement seems to be abandoned, based on the lack of lights inside the buildings. But I can sense the living beings who hide in these structures. They must be hoping I'll move on and leave them alone.

A figure jogs out of one of the buildings. The doors feature two halves that swing open and shut. As the person approaches me, I can tell it's a woman, since she wears a strange sort of dress that reveals most of her cleavage.

The female stops close to me, though not too close. "Hey, there, Mr. Demon. What can we do for ya tonight?"

"Who are you?"

"My name's Lucy. I own the saloon."

I have never heard of the term saloon. "Is this the Outlands?"

"Sure is, sugar. Don't see many dee—uh, folks like you 'round here."

"I am a demon. There's no need to pretend otherwise."

"May I, uh, ask your name? We're all real curious about you."

"I am Zaen'imuth, son of Zor'imuth, and true crown prince of the underworld."

Lucy's eyes almost bulge out of their sockets. "You're his kid? Wow, you must be the new king, then. We don't get much news way out here."

I clench my teeth. "I am not the king. The usurper Rahn'omith has stolen the crown from me. I seek vengeance."

"Yeah, 'course ya do. Not sure how the Outlands can help. We might be consigned to this place, but we ain't got magic powers."

"I am aware of that fact. I require information, not magics."

Lucy moves closer, and now I can see faint wrinkles around her eyes. "What do you need to know, hon?"

"Where to find the mortal woman who destroyed my father."

She winces and wrings her hands. "Whatcha want with her? She's nothing special. If you're needing a little power boost, I can help ya out with that. Your daddy liked to visit my establishment now and then to beef up his magics. I might be only a mortal, but I've got the juice you need."

"Just tell me the name and location of the woman who murdered my father."

"Well, uh...That might be a slight problem. See, the Outlands exists in the past. That girl ain't been born yet."

Time travel? I hadn't intended to hide this far back in time, and I have no idea why that happened. "Tell me the murderer's name. I will hunt her down by supernatural means."

"Um...okay." Lucy wraps her arms around herself and bites her lip. "Her name is Kylie Drummond. I think she lives in Utah, near the butte that used to be holy to the Kevitash tribe until—Never mind."

"Until what? Do not hold out on me. I have no patience for it."

"It's just that your daddy... Well, he kinda wiped out the Kevitash. Every last one of 'em is dead and buried."

I grasp her upper arms and drag her closer. "Tell me where to find this Kylie Drummond."

Lucy shrugs, but her lips are trembling. "Sorry, I can't. Told you everything I know about her. Well, except for—"

The wench tries to back away, but my hands restrain her.

I give her a hard shake and snarl, "Tell me everything."

"Kylie left with the sheriff. Ain't seen either of them since. We were all kinda gone for a while, until you showed up. Reckon we were stuck in limbo or something."

"Who is the sheriff?"

"Used to be Nathaniel Fortescue, back when he was a werewolf. No idea if he still is one."

I release her arms. "Good girl. Now tell me where to find the wolf."

"He'd be wherever Kylie is, I reckon. That's all I know, I swear."

Somewhere in Utah live a werewolf and his mate. However long it takes, whatever means I must employ, I will hunt down Kylie Drummond and Nathaniel Fortescue. No one kills a demon king and gets away with it.

"What you gonna do to those two?" Lucy asks. "Your daddy was a mean old cuss, and he didn't give that girl any other way out."

"The demon king owns the Outlands. That means everyone within its confines is enslaved to the king. You are all his property." I grind my teeth so hard that I'm sure Lucy can hear it. "But the throne should be mine."

The wench's face has become paler. "I'm sure you're right."

"What I seek is elsewhere. I must go now."

"But you'll be back, won't ya?"

"If Rahn'omith should come to this place, tell him nothing. I was never here. Understand?"

She nods.

I spread my arms, tip my head back, and summon the power I need to accomplish my task, though doing so drains me more than it should. *Take me to the wolf and his mate, I command the magics. Take me to Kylie Drummond and Nathaniel Fortescue.* I close my eyes and allow the dark energies to seep into my skin. They delve deeper still, burrowing through flesh and sinew and bone until the spell has infiltrated every molecule. The power invigorates me. My cock stiffens, though I have no intention of bedding a female. I'm saving this power for the two beings who must be destroyed.

When I open my eyes, I discover a portal is hovering five paces away from me. I push past Lucy and stride into the opening. The portal slams shut behind me.

Darkness. Peppered with lights. Far away. That's all I see.

The energy from the portal fed me even more power, and I break into a sprint of such speed that no mortal could even see me. I race onward, sniffing the air as I go, waiting to stumble onto the right scent. Strange noises assail me. They fade away so quickly that I don't even bother to wonder what they signify.

Then it happens. I smell...them.

My spell has done its job. It brought me to the wolf and his mate. But where am I? And where are they?

My sense of smell isn't as acute as that of a werewolf, so I need to move slowly while I wend my way toward my destination. Can't risk following the wrong scent. Once I reach the complex of buildings that must be a city, I move even more slowly. I stop, sniff the air, stop, sniff, repeating that action countless times before the magics I ingested point me to the right location.

Now I stand on a road that has been covered with a firm black substance. Yellow and white lines painted on the surface seem to delineate the sections of the road. Tall poles with bright lights attached to their tops illuminate the vicinity. How convenient. I won't need to test my night vision after all.

The structure in front of me looks like...a house.

As I sneak up to the structure and walk around its perimeter, I can see well enough in the dark to determine what's inside the house. In one room, a man and woman lie in bed together, sleeping. That would be Kylie Drummond and Nathaniel Fortescue. But in the other bedroom, I see a crib with a baby slumbering inside it. I open the window and climb inside without making a sound. Then I approach the crib, gazing down at the tiny girl. She has a smattering of dark hair.

Her scent makes me feel...protective.

No, I don't care about this child or her parents. That was a fleeting sensation. But I have found my way to exact vengeance. This will be even better than my original plan.

Because it hinges on this tiny babe.

CHAPTER TWO

Charlotte

HAPPY BIRTHDAY TO YOU. HAPPY BIRTHDAY TO YOU. HAPPY BIRTHDAY, dear Charlotte, happy birthday to you." My parents finally stop singing and start clapping instead. Mum and Dad go overboard sometimes, especially on birthdays, but I've gotten used to it after twenty-three years on earth. Then Mum says, "Sweetie, it's time to blow out the candles. If you wait any longer, they'll be wax puddles on the cake."

I take a deep breath and snuff out the candles.

My parents clap and cheer. Older people can be so strange. Mum might only be forty-eight, and Dad is only fifty-one, but they're older than I am which makes them older people. Despite their sometimes-embarrassing behavior, I love them to bits. I'd been worried that an outdoor birthday do would end in calamity, thanks to the wind that had picked up earlier. But it died down just in time for my celebration. Not only have I turned twenty-three today, but I've also found a job as a schoolteacher.

I glance around the lawn, pretending to be insulted. "Aren't there any presents?"

"You want gifts?" Dad says. "Awfully demanding, aren't you?"

"I seem to recall you and Mum saying I deserved to be pampered and given anything I wanted."

Mum rolls her eyes. "When you were six years old. I could go grab your old rattle and wrap it up quick."

"No thank you. But if you'd like to give me a fit, clever man for my birthday..."

Dad shakes his head and smirks. "Kylie darling, how did we raise such a cheeky chit?"

"No idea. It must've been your dormant werewolf genes that did it."

"Of course. Blame the man who was cursed."

Mum pokes him in the side. "It's been more than two decades since you were a wolf, so you can't trot out that excuse anymore."

No other family on earth would have this sort of discussion. As far as I know, there aren't any werewolves in England or anywhere in the world. My father had been cursed by a Rom witch who was forced to do it by Dad's evil uncle. Only one other wolf existed, apparently, and she was a bloody awful woman. Cordelia Atherton deserved to die.

Mum and Dad exchange secretive smiles. Then he races over to the bushes that flank the porch steps. He returns carrying two boxes and sits down beside Mum again. "Here are your gifts, pet. Your mother and I chose them, and we hope you'll appreciate what we've given you."

"Of course I will." I take the boxes he offers me and set about ripping them to shreds. I lift the item out of the first box. "Oh, this is lovely. But you can't give this to me. It belongs to you and Mum."

"That medallion saved our lives. It's a family heirloom now, and we want you to keep it. Please, love, accept this gift. It will make us very happy."

"Thank you. This is an amazing gift."

I lift the silver chain, letting the medallion dangle. It used to have a hemp cord. My parents must have upgraded it to silver just for me. They've told me the story about this piece of jewelry, but I never imagined they would give it to me considering how much it means to them. The bronze disk is the size of an American silver dollar. A breeze wafts over the lawn, causing the medallion to rotate slowly, back and forth, revealing both faces. One side features an image of a five-pointed star while the other bears the image of a howling wolf.

A strange sensation shivers through me, raising the hairs at my nape.

Mum reaches out to touch my hand. "Are you okay, Charlotte?"

"What? Oh, yes, I'm right as rain. Just can't believe you two are giving me this medallion. Does it still have magic in it?"

"No, the supernatural powers got drained from it a long time ago. Your father's last trip back to the past sapped it all. Now, it's just a cool old keepsake."

I lay the medallion on my palm, closing my fingers around it. "Thank you so much for this. It's amazing."

Dad nods toward the other box, which I had opened but not looked inside. "Go on, you've got one more present."

I rifle through the tissue paper inside the container until I find a small satin box. When I flip up the lid, my jaw drops. "Diamond earrings? These must have cost a ruddy fortune."

"Nothing is too good for you, pet."

Mum leans forward, pointing at the earrings. "Those are one carat stones with rose gold. Every woman should have a pair of diamond earrings."

I set down the medallion and put on the diamond studs. "How do I look?"

My father grins. "Positively smashing."

He used to be quite serious, but I think age has made him somewhat softer. When I was a little girl, he would play with me out on the lawn or in the drawing room. But he never grinned. We had fun together, though. Mum was always the one making silly choo-choo noises or blowing raspberries on my belly. I've been a bit spoiled as the only child of a wealthy earl and his countess.

My father whistles loudly.

And a trio of musicians rushes out of the solarium. They begin to play a waltz for us.

Dad rises and offers me his hand. "May I have this dance, Lady Charlotte?"

I can't help grinning, and I might be blushing a touch too. But I take my father's hand while he leads me around the lawn, teaching me how to waltz at the same time. After that, he dances with Mum. Their love for each other is visible and palpable, like a mystical force that binds them together. I've never seen another couple as devoted to each other as my parents.

Yes, I'm slightly biased.

Once my birthday festivities are over, I go into the drawing room to work out my lesson plans for tomorrow. Being a teacher at a community school isn't the most glamorous job for an earl's daughter, but my parents have never criticized my life choices. In fact, they've always encouraged me in whatever I chose to do. I am a good girl, always have been. That makes me rather boring, I imagine. Occasionally, I do wish I could break out of my mold and do something wild.

Oh, Mum would panic if she heard that. She worries about me—because she loves me. But she made the mistake of telling me once that she'd been dreaming of doing something wild herself when she met Dad. Can't erase that information from my mind.

Those thoughts spur me to shut my eyes and picture a tall, muscular man who whisks me away to an exotic place. The Caribbean, perhaps. Or possibly the South Pacific. I've never visited those places, but they've always intrigued me. As much as I love England, I would jump at the chance to travel abroad or even just in Europe. Honestly, Scotland would be wonderful too.

Anywhere just to experience more of the world.

By the time I've finished my lesson plans for tomorrow, it's still light enough out that I decide to go for a walk. I tell Mum and Dad about my plan, then head out to explore the Wilderhampton grounds, away from the house itself. All right, I might have neglected to tell my parents that I meant to go into the forest. A grown woman doesn't need permission. Just as I've reached the periphery of the trees, I change my mind. Might as well stick to the manicured grounds of Wilderhampton Manor. I have the medallion hanging around my neck, and I'm wearing my diamond earrings too. I love my birthday gifts, and I'd like to enjoy them for a bit longer before I put them in a safe place.

I've just turned around, heading back to the house, when a strange noise draws my attention. I halt and turn to look.

I can't see what made the noise. It almost seemed like...a growl.

Please don't tell me we have a werewolf on the premises.

A shadow shifts among the trees.

I shield my eyes with my hand, peering into the gloomy forest. "Who's there?"

Silence echoes back to me.

"Who are you?" I call out. "What do you want?"

My pulse accelerates. I clutch the medallion which feels oddly warm against my cool skin. Though I search the area again with my gaze, I can't see or hear anything. I imagined the noise, I suppose. But I still sense... I don't know. A presence. Nothing concrete.

I clench the medallion more firmly and call out again. "Show yourself."

No one answers. I wait another minute or two, but I don't hear anything else out there. So, I go back inside the house and get ready for bed. As I change into my satin chemise, I can't stop wondering about the incident out there in the forest. Had I imagined it? Maybe. But it had felt real. I try to forget about it, but even when I've settled in under the sheets, my mind keeps replaying those moments.

I pull the covers up to my chin.

Darkness falls over me. But the moon is full tonight. It has risen so high that the trees can't block it from my view. Yet a shadow does indeed blanket me. A shadow that moves. I spring upright, my heart racing. Bloody hell, what is wrong with me? I don't panic because a branch or something blocks the moonlight. But as I lean toward the window, I realize I've been wrong.

A manlike shape hovers there, dark and tall, its presence filling me with a sense of foreboding I've never experienced in my life.

My pulse pounds in my ears, as loud as a drumbeat. I leap off the bed and tear the door open. "Dad! Mum! Come quickly, someone is in my room."

A door bursts open down the hall. My parents are sprinting toward me.

When I glance at the little balcony again, the dark shape is gone.

Mum wraps an arm around me, pulling me close. "Nathaniel, go see what's in there."

"Please don't bother," I say. "I think it's gone, Mum."

The unease I'd felt a moment ago has indeed gone away. Yet I know someone or something had been there, hovering over me.

My father rushes to the balcony, flinging the glass doors open. He swivels his head this way and that, then stands perfectly still as only a former werewolf could do. Finally, he sighs and shuts the doors. As he returns to me and Mum, he shakes his head. "I saw nothing. Whatever it was is gone, Charlotte."

"You believe me that something was out there?"

Mum rubs her hands up and down my arms. "We will always believe you, sweetie. Considering our pasts, we never discount anything, no matter how weird it is."

"I'm so sorry I woke you both. Must've been a bad dream that seemed real."

No, I don't believe that. But I have no proof anything was in my room, and worrying Mum and Dad won't do any good.

And so, we all go back to bed. I fall asleep quickly but dream of a mysterious manlike shadow and that soft growling I'd heard in the forest. Oddly, those dreams don't disturb me. They make me feel sort of...aroused. But that's rubbish. I haven't had a good shag in months, and my subconscious gave me a steamy dream to alleviate the tension. If my parents knew I hadn't been a virgin since my first year at university, they might lock me up in Wilderhampton Manor and throw away the key. They're overprotective for a reason, but still.

I want to experience the world and all its pleasures.

The next morning, I rise and shine at seven o'clock precisely, feeling surprisingly good considering what happened last night. Mum and Dad say goodbye as I'm climbing into my car, headed to my school. I arrive ten minutes early, as usual, and get my classroom set up for the day. As much as I love teaching, it can be rather tedious. I try to come up with innovative ways to engage my students, yet I haven't done anything to engage myself—intellectually or otherwise. I've become stuck in a routine that leaves me less than satisfied.

Is this what my life will always be? Cafeteria lunch. Bad dates. Boredom.

There must be something else out there for me. Something exciting. A bloke who will thrill me and cherish me, a real man who knows how to treat a woman. I crave passion, the fiery sort that leaves a girl breathless.

No, I have never told my parents how I feel. I don't want to worry them.

At the end of the day, I walk out of my classroom feeling bloody good. My students always make me smile and laugh, and I do my best to give them the same thing. Yes, I do love my life.

And yet...I can't shake the feeling that something else is out there for me, something exciting, an experience that will change everything.

Most of the time, I don't drive directly home, and today is no different. Mum and Dad know I like to go shopping after work, even if all I do is window shop. So, I drive to Chelsea and the wonderful shopping district there. My mate Darcy, who works at the same school as I do, had wanted to come with me this afternoon, but she needed to take her daughter to the dentist. That leaves me alone to wander among the shops, gazing at things I will never buy. Yes, I can afford anything, thanks to my generous allowance from my parents, but I don't actually need a new dress that costs nine hundred pounds, do I? Of course not.

I've just rounded a corner, and I'm wondering if I should stop in at the café I can see further up the street, when I notice movement out of the corner of my eye. Someone has walked up behind me. I freeze for a moment, overcome by a sensation of déjà vu, as if I know the person who hovers behind me.

When I turn around, I realize the man is a complete stranger to me. So much for déjà vu. He towers over me, at least six inches taller than I am. My gaze wanders over the bloke›s body, from his broad shoulders to his muscular biceps that strain his T-shirt, and straight down to the significant bulge in his trousers. Good heavens, I have never seen a trouser snake that large.

"Are you having lunch at this establishment?" the man asks. "If you're alone, we could share a table. Then neither of us will be pathetically alone."

I can't share a meal with a total stranger, can I? An American, no less. He speaks in a stuffy way, using words like "establishment," and I can't deny that's endearing. Well, it isn't as if we would be alone in a vacant castle in Transylvania. Why shouldn't I enjoy lunch with a handsome stranger? "All right, that does sound lovely. Let's share a table. I'm Charlotte, by the way."

He holds out his arm as if he wants me to wrap mine around it. "I am Zane."

My gaze is drawn upward, to his eyes, and a chill shivers up my spine. His reddish-brown irises remind me of Scotch whisky. Despite that shiver, I accept his arm. When my bare skin touches his, I barely manage to stifle a gasp.

Then Zane aims his eerie eyes at me, and I forget why I shouldn't go with him.

CHAPTER THREE

Zane

I PULL OUT A CHAIR FOR CHARLOTTE AND PUSH IT BACK IN ONCE SHE sits down. This is what human males do, apparently. I had been holed up in a hotel for several weeks before I finally ventured out to find Charlotte. I needed to know about this world, else she might realize I'm not a normal man. After a great deal of chanting, I'd managed to cast a spell to cloak my true appearance. My red skin would have given away the game. By the time Charlotte realizes a demon has captured her, she won't be able to escape me.

Seduction is the most insidious means of capturing prey. I need to corrupt this woman so thoroughly that her loved ones won't recognize her, and she will become a willing servant to my voracious appetites, a wanton bound to me forever.

I smile at Charlotte the way men in Hollywood films do when they want to seduce a woman. Charlotte gives me an odd look. I must not be doing this correctly. Beguiling a mortal must be quite different from the way demons acquire sexual partners, and I might need to adapt my strategy.

"Where are you from?" Charlotte asks. "America, I assume, based on your accent."

"Yes, I am American." But I won't tell her that I studied Hollywood films and television shows to become American. I also learned something about her during my studies. "You are British, aren't you?"

"That's right. Are you on holiday?"

"Yes. I arrived yesterday, but I haven't had a chance to see the sights yet."

She bites her upper lip as her brows draw together. "You seem awfully anxious. If you're shy, don't worry. I won't bite, I promise."

But I might. The thought of sinking my teeth into the silky, glistening flesh between her folds... "Don't worry, Charlotte, I am not shy or anxious."

She puckers her lips, seeming confused, then shrugs and picks up a menu.

I also study my menu, but the only item I recognize is fish and chips. Based on my research, I know that means fried breaded fish with fried strips of potatoes.

The waiter arrives, and I order fish and chips.

Charlotte smiles and laughs, then turns to the waiter. "I'll have the same, please."

Once the boy has left, I must ask a question. "Why did you laugh when I ordered fish and chips? You wanted the same thing."

"Yes, but you seemed so unsure of yourself, almost as if you'd never seen that sort of food before. Or any food."

I am not unsure of myself. She has no idea how I behave when I'm not putting on an act to seduce her. I pick up my water glass and swallow half of it in one go.

Charlotte laughs again. "You're very strange, but I think that's adorable."

"Adorable?"

"It means your strangeness is endearing."

"Oh, I see." I push my chair back. "Would you excuse me for a moment? I need to use the restroom."

She watches as I saunter into the enclosed portion of the establishment. Once I turn down the narrow hallway that leads to the restrooms, I can't see Charlotte anymore. I enter the cramped restroom and check that no one else is in here, then barricade the door with the handle of a mop I'd found in the corner. I close my eyes and chant the appropriate words in the language of my demon clan. Time slows, and finally halts.

And a wizened hag appears before me. "In need of my services again so soon?"

Many moons have come and gone since I last needed the help of the demon sorceress Mazdala. But that is irrelevant. "I must understand this world immediately. Several weeks in a hotel room did not provide enough information."

She taps one of her long, black talons on my chest. "Always in a hurry, aren't you, Zaen'imuth? Sorcery requires finesse, not brute strength."

I grind my teeth. "I know that. Can't you speed up the process?"

"There will be a cost. Magics are never free, and I do not mean monetarily."

"No more cryptic statements. Tell me what you can do."

She circles around me twice before halting again directly in front of me. "To give you the knowledge that any mortal would have gained during an entire lifetime? I cannot even guess what the toll will be. Do you still want to do this?"

"Yes. Right now."

"As you wish."

Mazdala waves for me to back away. Then she spreads her arms and begins to chant in a tongue so ancient that it has no name. Energy sizzles over my skin and dives deep beneath my flesh to infiltrate every cell in my body. I gasp, then I can't breathe at all anymore. I fight the impulse to struggle against the spell, though I feel as if I might collapse and die. But an immortal such as I cannot be killed so easily.

The sorceress releases her magics.

And I can breathe again. I suck in a lungful of air.

"It is done," she says. "Use your knowledge well."

The sorceress vanishes.

She granted me what I asked for, yet I feel no different. Perhaps it won't kick in until I see Charlotte again. I race through the interior portion of the café but slow down as soon as I walk out onto the patio. The woman I seek remains in the chair she›d sat in since we entered the café. Now, though, she gazes down at the food on her plate. Why isn›t she eating? That›s what mortals do when they receive a meal.

I settle onto my chair. "Do you not like the food?"

Charlotte's head pops up. "What? Oh, no, I'm sure it's quite good. But I was waiting for you to come back."

"Why?" The moment I speak that word, a strange sensation floods through me, and suddenly, the right words tumble from my lips. So, I lean forward and touch her hand. "I'm glad you waited for me. Now, we can enjoy our meals together and talk too. I want to know everything about you."

"I'm not that interesting."

"Of course you are." I lift her hand, kissing the knuckles. "Charlotte, you are the most beautiful woman I've ever met. Your smile could light up the whole world, and your eyes are the most enchanting combination of hazel and blue. I have never seen such stunning irises before."

Her eyes widen. "What happened while you were in the loo? No more awkward Zane. You're suddenly a smooth talker."

"Your beauty threw me off kilter at first." I kiss her knuckles again and brush them over my cheek. "I apologize for my rude behavior. Can you forgive me?"

When I release her hand, she smiles shyly. "Yes, I forgive you. Shall we eat? I'm quite hungry."

"I'm ravenous too. We should order dessert once we've devoured our fish and chips."

Charlotte smiles again, but this time the shyness has faded away. "That's a brilliant idea, Zane."

Fish and chips do not look particularly appealing, but I eat them anyway and put on a rather convincing show of loving them. Charlotte clearly does enjoy eating flaccid planks of fried fish. Perhaps it's a meal the British people like but no one else does. Halfway through our meal, Charlotte begins to tell me about her family.

"Mum is American like you, but she married my father, who's British and an earl."

"What is an earl?"

"It means that Dad is officially called Lord Wilderhampton because he's the Earl of Wilderhampton. But his actual name is Nathaniel Fortescue."

My hand is resting on my thigh, and my fingers instinctively curl into a claw-like gesture. To hear the name of the wolf who helped destroy my father... I don't know if I can contain my anger. But Charlotte isn't done yet.

"You see, Mum and Dad met at an Old West ghost town in Utah that's a tourist attraction. I came along one year later." She laughs softly, and her eyes glitter in the sunlight. "My parents didn't really date. They met and shagged and got married."

"Shagged?"

"It's British for, um..." Charlotte glances around furtively, then slants toward me to whisper, "Having sex."

My cock twitches. For a demon, it doesn't take much to get aroused. But the thing that bothers me right now is my reaction every time she smiles or laughs. It gives me a strange feeling in my chest. This woman is my enemy. I must avenge my father's death, and she is the tool I will use to do that. Charlotte Fortescue means nothing else to me.

Defiling her in body and soul will do far more damage to Nathaniel Fortescue than simply beheading him would. By the time I've finished with Charlotte, her family won't recognize her.

"Are we ordering dessert, then?" she asks. "I saw Battenberg cake on the menu. Oh, I do love that."

I catch sight of a waiter and wave him over here. "We want two slices of Battenberg cake."

"Yes, sir, right away."

What is Battenberg? I have no idea. Any sort of dessert will be a new experience for me, but that hardly matters. Food in the underworld isn't designed to taste good. It exists only to provide minimal nutrition. Since fish and chips had underwhelmed me, I doubt any sort of cake will make me feel anything but full.

As the waiter sets our plates down on the table, Charlotte rubs her palms together and licks her lips.

I want to gorge myself on those lips, the ones on her face and the ones nestled between her creamy thighs. My breaths grow heavier. My cock throbs. When she gently sinks her fork into the pink and yellow flesh of the cake, sliding it onto her tongue, she moans with pleasure.

And I fist my hands on my thighs.

Charlotte spears a larger piece of cake, thrusting it into her mouth. She chews languorously this time, shutting her eyes. When she rests a hand on her collarbone, I grip the edges of my chair so tightly that I might have drawn blood. A soft growl emerges from me.

She freezes with her mouth open, a bite of cake on her fork as it hovers between her lips. Charlotte sets down her fork. She tips her head to the side. "Did you just growl at me, Zane?"

"No, I—It was my stomach making that noise."

"But you just ate fish and chips. How can you be so hungry already?"

I'm hungry for you, I think but don't say. Demons aren't known for our restraint, sexually or in any other way. But I've made a mistake, allowing my ravenous desire for her body to bleed into our conversation. I have only one option. "I apologize for my rude behavior. Please forgive me, Charlotte."

She shrugs. "Whatever. Eat your cake, and maybe your tummy won't growl anymore."

While the woman I need to fuck continues to daintily enjoy her cake, I must summon all my willpower to seem like a normal man enjoying a dessert. I want to shove the entire slice of cake into my mouth and wolf it down like a wild animal devouring its prey.

Charlotte wipes her mouth as daintily as she had eaten the cake, then sets her napkin down. "It was lovely meeting you, Zane. But I need to go home."

"You can't leave yet." I'm snarling at her now. Why can't I control my emotions? The sorceress had cast a spell to make me behave like a mortal.

"I can leave whenever I like." Charlotte rises from her chair. "Goodbye, Zane. This should cover my part of the bill."

She slaps a few pound notes on the table, then stalks off down the street.

I know those are pound notes, yet I can't figure out how to ensnare Charlotte. This will not do. I need to reconsider my tactics—and interrogate Mazdala. I try to teleport myself directly to my hotel room, so I can summon the sorceress in private, but I land somewhere else entirely.

The underworld.

Before I can get my bearings, two demons clamp their fists around my biceps. I stand at the base of the throne dais. The stench of blood wafts around me. The creature who sits on the throne gazes down at me with disdain.

"Zaen'imuth, kneel before your king."

"I will not. You are a usurper, Rahn'omith. My father was assassinated, which means I am the true king. You must honor the lineage."

He chuckles. "Are you expecting demons to be honorable? That is the most amusing thing I've ever heard."

I grind my teeth, struggling against the urge to leap onto the dais and rip Rahn's head from his body. "I am owed the kingship."

"You are owed nothing."

Though I despise needing to acquiesce even a little, I must do so now. Once I've reclaimed what I'm owed, I will toss this reptile into the deepest pit of hellfire and watch him burn into ash. "Since there is a dispute, we must have the hordes vote on the new king."

Rahn'omith throws his head back and roars with laughter. "Your stupidity amuses me, Zaen. But your fate was decided the instant your father was incinerated by a human female. I've wanted to rid the underworld of you for millennia, but Zor'imuth protected you. Not because he cared for you. Oh, no, he simply enjoyed torturing you for eternity. That is why he made you general of the collective demon armies."

I had already known that. I despised my father, and the only thought that kept me going for all those millennia was the knowledge that I would ascend the throne. I clench my fists so tightly that the veins in my arms bulge. "Rahn, you are a throne thief. Surrender the crown and declare me king, or I shall exterminate you the way the wolf destroyed my father."

"I grow tired of this conversation." He claps his hands, and the other demons rush to surround me. "You will never ascend the throne. But I must be rid of you right now. Seize him!"

The demons of my own horde charge at me with their teeth gnashing and saliva dribbling from their mouths. Members of numerous hordes from throughout the underworld join in, salivating at the chance to murder me. I invoke my darkest powers, teleporting out of the underworld and straight to the one place where the usurper and his minions cannot find me.

Just as I vanish, I hear Rahn'omith scream with rage.

He assumed I am as mindless as the rest of the hordes. That was his first mistake.

At least I still have powers with which to defend myself. I tip my head back to gaze up at the sky. This is the mortal world.

As I turn in a circle, I take note of the land and its features. The butte my father had often spoken of hunkers as a dark mass on the desert floor. I have come to Utah, though I'm uncertain of how to pronounce the name. This part of Utah once belonged to a native tribe known as the Kevitash. My father eradicated them long ago.

A breeze ruffles my hair. The scent of something I've not smelled in ages teases my senses. No, it can't be. But it is. I have caught the scent of...woman.

"Zaen'imuth," the breeze whispers. "Son of the demon king, listen to us."

"Who are you?" I whirl around. "Where are you? Who risks my wrath by annoying me in this way?"

"Snarl all you like, Zaen'imuth. We have been waiting for you, and your fate is ours to decide."

"Who are you?" I snarl again. "Cease these games and show yourself, you coward."

"No games. We are the Kevitash."

"You lie. The Kevitash tribe vanished ages ago."

A blast of wind hits me so hard that I stumble backward and just manage to catch myself before I fall down on my backside. "Tell me what you want. Tell me now."

"Or what? You have no power over us."

I suck in a deep breath and bellow, "Leave this place now!"

"We cannot do that. Your journey is about to begin. Do not waste this chance, for you will never receive another."

"No more riddles. They mean nothing."

"You will understand soon enough. Good luck, Zaen'imuth, you will need it."

While the wind subsides and silence descends upon the earth, I shuffle down the path where a street had once been. The buildings that had once stood tall on either side of the street have completely vanished, absorbed by the magics that eradicated my father.

A strange sensation rushes over my skin from head to toe. The hairs at my nape tingle and stiffen. I halt, crouching to study the bare earth. As I run my fingers over the dirt, a much stronger tingling sensation burrows beneath my skin, straight down to my bones.

I drop to my knees, my hands flat on the ground, and lower my head to sniff the dirt. *Blood*. Not merely blood, but the life essence of a demon—of my father. I shut my eyes and inhale deeply. Yes, this is the location where Zor'imuth died. The wolf's mate destroyed him.

Nathaniel Fortescue and his woman must die.

The earth beneath me shivers and slithers. A vague outline begins to surface. Then it gradually resolves into a shape I recognize.

A sheriff's badge.

I try to snatch it up, but the badge disintegrates. The Kevitash are determined to torment me, but I am not so easily disturbed. Perhaps I did hate my father, but I cannot allow his death to remain unavenged. How will I punish the wolf and his mate? I have pondered that question often lately without reaching a conclusion. As I amble down the path that had once been a street, the solution to my dilemma crystallizes in my mind.

I will take the wolf's daughter and ruin her.

But first, I must do something else. Every demon needs a lair and acolytes. I cannot return to the underworld, so my lair in that domain is out of reach for now. I spread my arms wide, tipping my head back to gaze directly at the full moon. Its milky light seeps under my skin, invigorating my powers. "Rise from the ashes, my kindred travelers. Rise and bow down before me."

The wind whips up again, stronger than before, whirling like a tornado and roaring like a ravenous beast. The gale lashes my hair to my face. I summon all the demonic energy I can muster and chant in the old language while a racket erupts around me. I can't see what's happening, but I feel it. And within a single moment, it is done.

Silence returns. A slight breeze kisses my skin.

I lower my arms and smile. Perhaps I am no longer the favored son of the demon hordes, but my powers have not diminished too much. I tip my head back and wink at the moon. Before me lies a town of the sort mortals refer to as the "Wild West," I believe. The seedy settlement houses gamblers, whores, and miscreants of every variety. These people will be my acolytes.

When I visited this place the first time, it had been forlorn and forgotten. But I have resurrected the town and its denizens.

The residents pivot their heads in my direction, clearly confused, and shuffle out onto the street to make their way toward me. Soon, a crowd has gathered before me.

"I have resurrected the Outlands," I declare. "But this is not the old town you knew. This one exists in a parallel realm beyond time and space. No mortal may see or enter the Outlands without my permission."

Lucy brazenly approaches me. Her blonde hair has streaks of gray in it, and her face exhibits faint wrinkles around her eyes and mouth when she smiles. "I'll serve you any way ya like, big man. And I do mean *any* way."

"A harlot's body is of no interest to me." But I suddenly realize she can assist me in another way. "I am now the sheriff of this land, and you shall be my deputy."

"Me? I don't know nothin' about the law."

"There is no law here except for my edicts. You will follow my commands precisely."

"You know I will." She lays her hands on my chest. "I've had all kinds of men, but never one whose skin was as red as a sunset."

I grasp her wrists, peeling her hands away. "Do not touch me. I will never take your body, you ignorant wench."

"Mind if I call you Zane?"

This woman annoys me intensely. But I do need a right-hand, and she seems eager to please me. "Yes, you may call me Zane."

I might as well get used to my pseudonym. I need a human-style name.

A young man approaches us, haltingly at first, then more swiftly as he stops beside Lucy. "I want to serve you too, Zane. Please. Let me help."

"What is your name?"

"Cooper."

"I hereby deputize you, Cooper. Lucy is first in command, after me, and you shall be second deputy."

He grins. "Thanks a lot, Zane."

Despite the friendliness of these people, I know they are not quite human anymore. They had been banished to the Outlands because they are depraved and amoral. But these are precisely the sort of beings I need in my army. To annihilate Rahn'omith, crown thief, will require a battle. My plan ends with his destruction, but it begins with vengeance for my father's death.

That is how I will establish my dominance.

"Prepare this town," I tell Cooper and Lucy. "The daughter of the wolf will arrive soon. I need only retrieve her."

Cooper raises his hand. "Uh, do you mean you're kidnapping her?"

"What else would I mean? I will kill the wolf and steal his daughter."

The crowd abruptly parts, and even Lucy and Cooper move to the side to accommodate the woman who saunters toward me. She wears a long, flowing black dress adorned with beads that click as she moves. A scarf covers her hair, and a ring adorns her right middle finger.

She halts before me. "I am Kezia of the Rom, cast into the Outlands for my wickedness. Now, I serve you, Zane. And I have seen the future."

I fold my arms over my chest as I study the woman. "If you know something—"

"Of course I know something." She stretches her arms up to grasp my face. "The wolf has become a mere mortal, and his mate is no longer invested with magics. Nathaniel Fortescue and his bride, Kylie, cannot give you what you need."

"And I suppose you know how to rectify the situation."

"Indeed I do." Her bare feet lift off the ground as she rises to stare into my eyes. "What you seek now is the daughter of the wolf, Charlotte Fortescue."

A tingle sweeps over my skin, lifting every hair, and my pulse accelerates. My breaths grow shallower. "You can find Charlotte for me?"

The gypsy lowers herself onto the ground and takes two steps backward. "Yes, my lord, I will send you directly to her."

Charlotte. The name echoes in my mind even as my body awakens, enlivened by the prospect of defiling the daughter of the wolf and making her my queen. She is a luscious female ripe for the taking. "Will I defeat Rahn'omith and claim the throne that is rightly mine?"

Kezia shrugs. "That is up to you. But I will show you how to reach the daughter of the wolf."

Vengeance shall be mine—and so will Charlotte Fortescue.

CHAPTER FOUR

Charlotte

THE SUN BEAMS DOWN ON ME, WARMING MY FACE AND ENCOURAGING every muscle in my body to relax. Anytime the clouds disappear, I take the chance to revel in the lovely sunshine. Ahhh, this feels deliciously frivolous. I love it. But I sometimes wish I had a boyfriend who could share this feeling with me. My parents enjoy the sun too, though not as ardently as I do.

"Charlotte! We're having brunch on the patio."

Mum's voice snatches me out of my reveries. I yawn and shout, "Be there in a minute."

I stretch, yawn again, and finally rise. As I approach the patio, I notice Dad has only just now emerged from the solarium. My friends often ask me if it feels strange to live in a centuries-old house that has always belonged to the Fortescue family. Not all my ancestors were decent people. My grandfather Mordecai was evil, and I'm not exaggerating. He treated my grandmother horribly and my father too. Then my uncle Archibald turned my father into a werewolf.

The strangest part of my family history is that my father was born in the nineteenth century. He met my mum back then too, though she was from the twenty-first century. It's all bloody confusing.

Dad and I are apparently the only decent members of the Fortescue family.

My parents are already seated at the patio table when I drop onto my chair. I study the food laid out on platters and in dishes. "Ooh, this looks yummy. We haven't had a good fry up in ages."

Dad aims a sly glance at Mum. "Your mother thinks too many fry ups might clog my arteries. I keep telling her that if I could survive being turned into a wolf, my body can handle anything."

We never discuss the truth about our family's past in front of anyone else, not even the few employees who live and work at Wilderhampton Manor. If we started talking about my grandfather who died two hundred years ago, we would all end up in an asylum.

Do they have have those anymore?

Once we've all started eating, I decide now is the right time to broach a subject they probably won't like. Who am I kidding? They'll freak out, as Mum would say. But it's now or never. "Um, I was thinking of taking a holiday in America. Darcy, Amelia, and Eden suggested we should go there to see where I was born and to have a good time."

Dad drops his fork. It clatters on his plate. "You're too young to travel abroad."

"I'm twenty-three, for heaven's sake. That means I am an adult who doesn't need your permission. I'm being a good daughter and asking for your blessing instead of doing a runner."

When he opens his mouth to object, Mum lays a hand on his arm. "She's right, Nathaniel. Charlotte is old enough to make her own decisions. Besides, it's not like she wants to go to Burning Man."

Dad gawps at her. "Why would anyone want to watch a bloke being burned alive?"

Mum tries to stifle her laugh, but she ends up spluttering. "Burning Man is a festival-type thing out in the desert. I've never been there, but I hear it's pretty wild."

Before my father can object again, I hold up a hand. "I vow that I am not going anywhere near Burning Man."

Dad leans back in his chair, crosses his arms, and lifts his brows. "Where, then, are you going?"

"The western part of the United States."

"Being cagey won't convince me this holiday is a good idea."

Mum gives me her best skeptical look too. "I have to agree with your father on this one. What don't you want us to know?"

I slouch in my chair and bluster out a sigh. "We're going to Utah." I wince. "To the Wrathrock Ghost Town."

Dad snaps upright. "Why in the bloody hell would you want to go there?"

"Because I've never seen it, and the location has special meaning for our family. We moved away from Utah when I was just a baby." I lean forward and do my best to convince them. "Whether you like it or not, Wrathrock and the Kevitash butte are an integral part of our family history. Shouldn't I get to see it in person just once? With my mates. That way I won't be alone."

My father stares at me for so long that I think he might be contemplating whether to lock me in my bedroom for the next decade or so. Then his posture sags, and he clasps Mum's hand. "If you think we should let her go, I will agree."

Mum chews on her bottom lip. "Yes, I think we should let Charlotte do this. It's important to her, and we need to show our daughter that we trust her. She won't do anything reckless."

Dad looks at me. "When will you leave?"

"In two weeks." My heart skips a beat. I'm actually going to America. "Better start making all the reservations. Will you worry too much if we stay at the hotel in Fiara Flats?"

"Not at all. It's only the Outlands that would worry me, but you aren't going there. Fiara Flats is simply a town." He clasps Mum's hand again. "Would it bother you, love?"

"Nope. My paranormal adventure started there, but it wasn't the catalyst for any of the bad things that happened."

I glance back and forth between Mum and Dad. "There won't be any supernatural nonsense this time. The Outlands was demolished, so I will be perfectly safe in Utah."

We enjoy the rest of our brunch, and my parents tell me all about Utah—again. I've heard the story so many times, but I never get tired of hearing it. After the food is gone,

Mum and Dad go into the house. I grab my car keys and drive into London to do a bit of pre-holiday shopping. I need new outfits. New shoes too. Oh, and a new purse. My mates join me, and we have a wonderful time exploring fun little boutiques. We only buy what we'll need for our trip. I'm sure Dad would be stunned to find out we didn't "go hog wild," as Mum would say.

Two weeks later, our plane touches down in Utah.

We're exhausted after the long airline trip, despite traveling first class, so we head straight for our hotel in Fiara Flats. The time difference means we need one whole day to recover. But we booked this holiday for two weeks. That means we'll have plenty of time to explore the place of my birth.

On our second full day in America, we drive our hire car to Wrathrock.

We've just parked in the guest lot and are making our way out into the ghost town itself when a familiar someone trots over to us.

I throw my arms around her for a quick hug. "Jenna Foster? I can't believe we bumped into you here. I thought you were living in California these days."

"Yeah, I am. But your mom made me promise I'd check on you."

Of course Mum did. She worries too much.

"Well, I'm chuffed to see you, anyway," I tell Jenna. "You haven't been to Wilderhampton in at least a year. We all miss you."

"I miss you guys too. Megan wished she could come with me, but the poor girl had an appendectomy a few days ago. She sends her love."

"How awful. I hope she's all right."

"Don't worry about Megan. She's one tough chick." Jenna studies my mates. "These must be your friends. Kylie mentioned they'd be here with you, but I haven't met them yet."

"Oh, how rude of me. Please let me introduce you to my three best mates." I point to each woman in turn. "Darcy Adlington, Amelia Nolan, and Eden Smyth. We met at university and have been friends ever since."

"Kind of like me, Kylie, and Megan. It's great to meet you girls. May I show you around Wrathrock? I'm an expert on this place after all the times I babysat you, Charlotte, while your mom was busy tour-guiding."

That was before my father returned from the past. Since I don't know how much Mum told her friends, I'd better not mention anything about how Dad acquired all the money we have now. It involved Rom sorcery, after all.

With Jenna as our tour guide, we get an insider's view of the ghost town. It looks nothing like the way I imagined it would. But then, the version my parents had experienced had been a supernatural creation, not a normal town in the Wild West. Still, I enjoy the kitschy atmosphere. We even get to watch a silly recreation of a gunfight. Jenna laments the fact that the proprietor hasn't hired better actors, not even after decades in business.

I rather like the melodramatic silliness. It makes me laugh.

We stop in at the saloon to grab some bottles of water. The desert makes us thirsty. While we stand at the edge of the saloon's porch, I can't resist sweeping my gaze over the landscape, from the jagged mountains to the floor of the Great Basin on which Wrathrock and Fiara Flats lie. A breeze ruffles my hair, and the strands tickle my cheeks. I swear I can smell the desert, but that's barmy.

Something about this region gives me a feeling of déjà vu. I suppose that›s because I›ve heard all the stories my parents told me about this place and the people who lived here. But this isn't the Outlands. It's a cheesy ghost town. Still, Mum first met Dad here, sort of, when a shadowy cowboy figure lured her down an alley where a shaman of the Kevitash clan gave her a mysterious medallion.

If she had ignored the mirage-like figure, I wouldn't be here today.

Jenna leads us down the porch steps and toward the next building she wants to show us. As we pass by the alley, the hairs at my nape stiffen and prickle. My breaths quicken. I try not to do it, try so bloody hard, but I can't stop myself from swerving my head in the direction of the alley.

A figure stands there. Tall. Muscular. Shirtless.

Grit flies into my eye, triggering tears. I wipe them away.

The figure is gone.

I must have imagined I saw someone. Naturally, I would hallucinate seeing a man in that alley, for the simple reason that I know Mum walked in there all those years ago. Should I go down there? Absolutely not.

The shadow figure appears again. Something like a magnetic pull urges me to move, and the compulsion grows too strong, almost painful. I turn toward the alley and take one step. Then another.

A hand seizes my arm, halting me.

I blink swiftly, feeling a bit dazed.

Jenna wags a finger at me. "Oh, no, sweetie, you are not going in there. I'm under strict orders from your mom to keep you away from that alley."

She said I can't go down this alley, but she didn't mention any other ones in Wrathrock. That means I could—

"Don't even think about going down any other alleys," Jenna says. "Think of me as your bodyguard. I won't let you out of my sight, Charlotte."

"I am an adult, you know."

"Sure. But I have three kids which means I've got the mamabear instinct. Better stick to the main areas of Wrathrock, or else I'll have to take you girls back to your hotel."

"All right, you win. I won't go down any alleys."

Our trip to Wrathrock winds down shortly after the incident that I won't tell anyone about because it would sound barmy. As we climb back into our hire car and drive away, I twist my head around to stare out the back window. I don't see any mysterious figure emerging from an alley.

Had I imagined seeing that muscular stranger?

Darcy is driving, and Eden took the front passenger seat. That leaves me and Amelia in the back. But while my mates enjoy a good chin wag, I find myself lost in thought, remembering that shadow figure and the strange excitement I'd experienced when I spotted him. Then he'd vanished. It must have been an illusion. No one would walk down an alley in a tourist town while half-naked. I couldn't even see the person's face.

Our hotel includes a restaurant, so we decide to have dinner there. We ask for a table that offers a bit of privacy, and the maître d› escorts us to a curved booth in the corner. Once we've all sat down, my mates give me odd looks. They must have noticed my distracted state.

"Are you all right, Charlotte?" Eden asks. "You've been preoccupied all day."

Darcy nods. "Oh, yes, she definitely has been somewhere else. Don't you agree, Amelia?"

"Absolutely. Charlotte did seem to have fun at first, but then she started glancing here, there, and everywhere as if she were waiting for someone."

Eden rubs her palms together. "Ooh, maybe she was waiting for her hot American lover."

Darcy snorts. "Then he's a tosser. She didn't meet anyone in that dusty ghost town."

"None of the above," I pronounce. "You lot have watched too many soap operas."

Fortunately, the waiter arrives to take our orders. Then the conversation turns away from me. We discuss where we should go tomorrow to continue our Utah adventures.

"Let's go to the Kevitash butte," I suggest. "That place has special meaning for my family. I am part-Kevitash, after all, on my mother's side."

"Did you ever get one of those home DNA tests?" Darcy asks. "You're probably one-twenty-fifth Kevitash. That's not enough to make me want to slog across the desert to stare up at some giant rock."

"It's not simply a rock. It's a butte."

"What's the difference? I'm no geologist, and neither are you."

Eden slings an arm across my shoulders and gives me a quick squeeze. "If it means that much to Charlotte, we should go there."

My two other friends exchange glances, then voice their agreement.

The next morning, we climb into our vehicle and head out. Fortunately, I'd bought a map when we picked up our car the other day, so I'm fairly certain I can get us to the butte. A tingle of excitement sweeps through me.

I'm about to step onto the land of my ancestors.

CHAPTER FIVE

Zane

YESTERDAY, I HAD ALLOWED CHARLOTTE FORTESCUE TO SEE ME, though only for a moment. That glimpse hadn't lasted long, yet she seemed unperturbed by the brief encounter. She has no idea who I am, or what I intend to do to her. On that night when I stood over sweet little Charlotte's crib in her parents' home, I had experienced a sudden insight. I knew what I must do to avenge my father's murder.

And Charlotte is the key.

The broad scope of my plan required that I garner as much information as I could about Kylie, Nathaniel, and little Charlotte. I doubt any demon has ever attempted such a wide-ranging, epic feat simply to punish another demon. Most of my kind are...not the smartest creatures in the multiverse. Rahn'omith is cunning, but not a genius. He will be too focused on cementing his power as the usurper king. That gives me plenty of time to enact my perilous plot.

I will bend time to my will.

Perhaps I've gone insane, for only a madman would attempt time travel. I might die in the process, but it will be worth the risk if I can pull off this feat. No other demon has ever even tried to do it. To gather all the information I need, I must begin where I left Charlotte—in that house, in the nursery. My first attempt at time travel went more smoothly than I could have hoped. The girl saw me, and she was intrigued. I've gone forward, but now it's time to bend the years backward.

To achieve this feat, I've come to the Kevitash butte. It rises perhaps five hundred feet from the desert floor and seems to have no entrance point. But I know there is one, and I find it easily. Only with careful observation can anyone discover the sliver of rock that protrudes from the massive rock formation, concealing the passage that lies behind it. Once I squeeze through it, I find myself inside a darkened passageway carved out of the butte itself. Mortals would need a torch to light their way, but I linger just inside the passage until my night vision is good enough to get me where I need to go. The passageway extends for about fifty paces. It ends at the opening of the Kevitash chamber. Images painted by the tribe eons ago decorate the walls.

Ah, but they are more than decorative. These images are alive.

Right now, they remain dormant. I have no need to activate the paintings, particularly since the Kevitash were never allies of the demons. They despised us. My father did cause the death of Erosabel, a woman of dual Kevitash and Rom heritage, who Zor'imuth coveted. She outwitted him, a fact I've always found amusing.

My father had his revenge, though. He destroyed the Rom witch.

Those are the tales my father told. He probably inflated them.

I care nothing about the fate of the Kevitash or the Rom. All I need from this chamber is the magics it holds, the kind that will grant me unlimited power. If I use the power properly. If I make a mistake, even a minuscule one, I might destroy myself and perhaps the entire multiverse.

Yes, time travel is that dangerous.

I squat on the floor, drawing a circle around myself in the dust. Then I straighten and begin to chant in the demon tongue. Magics lick at my skin. Soon, their interest grows more ardent, and they begin to nip at my flesh. As I reach the zenith of my chanting, the dark energies clamp down on me with the sharpness of dozens of knives. I grit my teeth and keep going. Just a little more...

The energies release their grip.

A breath blusters out of me. I wipe sweat from my brow while I wait for my pulse to slow. Have I amassed enough power? Now is the time to find out.

I close my eyes and formulate my command. *Take me to Charlotte Fortescue, the daughter of the wolf.*

A spinning sensation rocks me, and I struggle to remain on my feet. I must have plenty of power now, if the magics can push a demon like me off balance. Once the sensation fades, I open my eyes. Where am I? It's dark where I find myself now, and I need a brief moment to get my bearings. But I recognize this place. I'm in the nursery where I'd first seen baby Charlotte and conceived my plan. She isn't a tiny babe anymore, though. The daughter of the wolf has grown big enough that her old cradle stands empty in the corner, replaced by a bed just the right size for a somewhat older child.

I believe humans call them "toddlers."

Yes, I've learned much about this world in the thirteen years it took me to collect the magics and the knowledge I needed. I am in the past right now. As I kneel beside the bed, I can hear the faint susurrations of her breathing. A shaft of moonlight breaks through the clouds beyond the window, revealing the sweet, innocent face of Charlotte Fortescue. She has grown quite a bit, now almost as tall as my arm is long.

For a while, I kneel here watching the little girl sleep. I'm gathering more data, that's all. I have no feeling for this child. She is a means to an end, nothing more.

Suddenly, I realize the sun has risen. I can still see the moon, though it has become only a faint disk in the sky.

Then I hear footsteps outside the door to this room.

I sacrifice a small amount of magics to cloak myself—just in time. Someone is opening the door.

A woman enters the room and approaches the bed. She smiles down at Charlotte, then gives the child a gentle shake. "Time to wake up, sweetie."

The child opens her eyes and yawns.

Kylie Drummond picks her daughter up and heads for the doorway. She must be Kylie Fortescue now, since I assume she married the wolf. "Daddy made breakfast for us, Charlotte. Wasn't that sweet of him?"

The child gazes at something past her mother's shoulder. She stares at me and speaks one word. "Who?"

"What did you say, Charlotte?"

She thrusts a finger toward me. "Daddy?"

Kylie glances backward. "Daddy's not here. He's in the kitchen."

"Who?" The babe points at me again.

The mother and child disappear into the hallway.

Charlotte could see me, despite my cloaking spell. How strange.

I remain concealed as I follow the pair through the large house, down two flights of stairs, until we enter the dining room. I pay little attention to the conversation between Kylie and Nathaniel. The layout of the house does interest me. I need all the details I can gather about this family. When I had first found Charlotte, she and her parents had been living in Utah. Now, they clearly live somewhere else that has vastly different topography.

After breakfast, the little family moves into another room that has padded chairs, smaller tables, and a toy box. A small fire burns in the hearth. Kylie sets Charlotte down a reasonable distance from the fire, then leads her husband over to the television. She reaches for the remote control.

Nathaniel snatches it away from her. "I will do this."

Kylie smirks. "Okay, honey. Whatever makes you feel manly."

The former wolf struggles with the remote for several minutes, cursing under his breath many times. Finally, he tosses the device halfway across the room, where it whacks into the wall. "Damn it all to hell. I've become a foozler."

"You are not clumsy, but it's adorable when you start spouting Victorian slang." Kylie walks up to him and pats his chest. "Relax, honey. It'll take time for you to fully acclimate to the twenty-first century."

He sighs heavily, and his posture slumps. "But it's been two years. I should be accustomed to this world by now."

"You could always use the voice remote."

"That is not a helpful suggestion. The remote seems unable to understand my accent." Nathaniel pulls his wife into his arms and kisses her passionately. Then he leads Kylie over to the corner of the sitting room where Charlotte is playing with some sort of toys that have a square shape. "I still have seen no evidence of shifter qualities in Charlotte. Have you?"

"None whatsoever."

Kylie lifts Charlotte into her arms and kisses the child's forehead. The girl smiles and laughs, then stretches one little hand out to tap her father's lips. He taps her nose with one finger, which encourages her to smile.

"See?" Kylie says says. "She's perfectly normal. We've been through loads of lunar cycles, and absolutely zippo has happened."

I've just gained another morsel of information. Kylie and Nathaniel have worried that their daughter might become a werewolf. Why? I haven't yet been able to determine when precisely Charlotte was born. It might have been after her father became a normal human male, or it might have been before that. I need more data.

My thoughts consumed me so thoroughly that I abruptly realize the family has left the room. I hurry to catch up to them and realize I must have lost time. Charlotte and her parents are wearing different clothing, and the sun is out. I rush through the entire house, then spot the little family out on the lawn. I skulk out there, unsure of whether they will see me. They clearly do not. Charlotte is playing with blades of grass while her parents engage in conversation.

What interests me now is not the child's behavior. I hover behind the chairs on which Nathaniel and Kylie relax, and I listen to their exchange.

Nathaniel leans toward his wife to whisper, "I hope my past won't taint her."

"Taint who? Charlotte?"

"Yes."

"Don't be silly. Your dad was an asshole, but you are a wonderful man." Kylie lays a hand on his cheek and touches her lips to his. "Stop worrying so much."

"But I am...an incident."

Kylie struggles to stifle a laugh. "You're a what?"

"An incident." Nathaniel screws up his mouth, but then sighs with resignation. "It means I'm illegitimate."

"Oh, I get it. Your mom wasn't married when you were born, but that's not your fault." His wife pats his thigh. "Besides, like I've told you over and over, nobody in this century gives a hoot about that."

"I still have not fully acclimated."

"You'll get there. Give it time."

This family intrigues me more than I expected. I find myself trailing after the trio until evening, and I watch as Kylie and Nathaniel tuck their daughter in for the night and make their way across the hall to their spacious bedroom. I watch them undress, though I feel not even a twinge of titillation from observing them. Once they have settled in under the covers, Kylie initiates a conversation.

"You've been anxious lately. I'd like to know why." When he opens his mouth, she seals his lips with two fingers. "The real reason. No more 'I'm confused by the modern world' excuses. Confess, Nathaniel."

"As you wish." He toys with the strap of her chemise, clearly trying to distract himself. "I have suffered from unusual dreams of late."

"Tell me about them."

He avoids her gaze. "I have dreamed that Charlotte will become a wolf when she comes of age. She was conceived while I was still a werewolf, after all."

Kylie lays a hand on his cheek, urging him to look at her. "Oh, sweetie, that won't happen. Trust me."

"You can't possibly know that."

"I trust my motherly intuition. After everything you went through back in the Outlands, I get why you're freaking out over a few dreams. But our little girl will not become a shifter. I know that deep in my soul."

His eyes shimmer with what seems like the barest start of tears. But he rubs his eyes and unleashes a gusty breath. "Perhaps I am worrying too much."

"Would you rather fret or make love to me?"

Nathaniel's lips kink up at one corner. "I'm certain you know the answer to that question."

I decide not to spy on them while they make love and instead return to the nursery to observe the child sleeping. This is not giving me any additional data, though, and it serves no purpose for me. I invoke the magics once again, traveling further into the future—or rather, the past that has become the future for the duration of my exploratory mission.

The former werewolf sheriff of the Outlands worries that Charlotte might become a wolf herself. *Interesting.*

A few days at most have gone by, a fact I discerned based on the realization that Charlotte has not grown larger yet she sleeps in a different one-piece outfit than the one she'd worn before. I remained in the girl's bedroom while time sped forward. Since she still sleeps, I sneak across the hall and invoke a quick burst of extra magics to let me walk through the doorway. I shouldn't have wasted power on that, but I need to know what the wolf and his mate are discussing. I could hear their muffled voices when I stepped into the hall.

The couple lies in bed, and Kylie has just slid a hand down to Nathaniel's groin. The sheets cover their bodies, but her intent is obvious. She gives her husband a sly smile. "Good morning, Nathaniel."

"Good morning, love."

"You're still worrying about Charlotte, aren't you?"

Nathaniel winces. "Yes."

"Are you going to share your suspicions now?"

"I believe the dreams are suggesting that I must go back to where it all began. Where I began."

"We're already there. Wilderhampton is where you began."

"No, I was born in London. Remember?" He swipes a hand over his face. "But I'm speaking of where the new version of me came into being. That happened when I undertook my long journey from England to the Utah Territory. It's where I became the sheriff of a nameless town, a British werewolf in the Wild West."

"Well, I guess we can take a trip to Utah."

He sits up, gazing down at his wife. "No, love, I need to go back to the Outlands—back to the past."

"Oh." Her eyes flare wide. "You want to use the Kevitash medallion to travel back in time."

"Yes."

"No, Nathaniel, you can't do that. What if you aren't able to come home again?"

He lifts her onto his lap. "You and Charlotte mean everything to me. For our daughter, I must do this. To know for certain that she will not be cursed as I once was."

Tears shimmer in Kylie's eyes. She swallows hard enough that I can see the movement in her throat. Then she sniffles and wipes her eyes with the back of one hand. "I know you need to do this, and I can't go with you. But please, Nathaniel, come back to us. We need you."

"As I need you both." He grasps her face with both hands. "I vow I shall return."

Though I follow as they get dressed and head outside, I can't stop thinking about that phrase Kylie spoke—"Kevitash medallion." She stated that it has the power to send someone back in time. *Kevitash medallion.* Those words echo in my mind, over and over, like a bell ringing out the news. I have never heard of such a medallion. Yet if it does exist, I wonder if I could commandeer its power and add that to my own.

Nathaniel pulls the medallion out of his pocket and clasps it tightly.

The world shifts around us, and suddenly, I find myself inside the chamber within the Kevitash butte.

Nathaniel enters the chamber, blinking swiftly as his eyes adjust to the light.

On the chamber wall, the original Kevitash paintings have been replaced by a different story. The images animate themselves, depicting not a wolf, but a demon who pursues a small girl. She flees from the demon, and he seems about to catch up to her. She whirls around and throws one hand up.

The demon falls to the ground.

And the girl crouches over his limp form as if studying the beast. Then she rises and grows from a child to a woman. She is Charlotte Fortescue.

Her father stares at the images, which no longer move.

"Would you like me to explain the images to you?"

Nathaniel's brows cinch up, and his jaw slackens. He seems surprised that a demon would wear jeans and a black T-shirt. "Who are you? Not Zor'imuth. He is gone."

"I am Zaen'imuth, son of the demon king."

"Did you summon me to this place?"

"No. You brought yourself, and I'm taking advantage of your arrival." I lean against the wall, hooking one thumb inside my waistband. "I've come to deliver good news."

"A demon providing good news? You must assume I'm insane, for no rational person would believe your claim."

"I can tell you're skeptical, Nathaniel. But I have orders from on high, and I intend to fulfill them." I glance at the moving artwork on the wall, pretending that I caused them to be animated. I've also lied about having orders from on high. I need him to believe I'm still a part of the underworld. I wave toward the paintings. "This is a depiction of a true event that hasn't happened yet. The female in that painting is your daughter, Charlotte."

"You dare to speak my daughter's name?" Nathaniel snarls. "I shall wring your neck."

He leaps at me, intent on wringing my neck, but I whisk myself to the other side of the chamber.

I wag a finger at him. "Calm yourself, Nathaniel. I haven't come to threaten your family. On the contrary, I intend to protect them. The new king of the demon hordes has cast me out. The Kevitash spirits have commanded me to undertake a dangerous task for them."

"If I am to believe your claims, then one question remains. What does your task have to do with my child?"

"You will find out eventually." I bow deeply. "Return to your family now, and don't worry about the future."

I vanish, reappearing on the other side of the butte. My deceptions will keep Nathaniel and his family fixated on a fictional coup, waiting years for it to occur. Meanwhile, I will be focused on another task altogether.

Seducing Charlotte Fortescue.

But I have drained myself and need more energy to sustain me for this task. I have only one option. I must visit the Outlands and hope I can mine magics from the town or its residents. I use my last ounce of power to do that. The second I touch down on the dirt road, Lucy and Cooper race up to me.

"How'd it go?" Cooper asks.

"Where is Kezia?"

"The Rom woman?" Cooper shakes his head. "No idea."

"Can't never trust a Rom," Lucy declares. "They're slippery and sneaky."

As if she isn't. This is a town full of depraved characters. That's why my father created this place. He loved to watch mortals and demons alike rip each other to shreds in every way imaginable.

But I have no time to hunt for Kezia. So, I throw my head back and roar, "Where is the Rom witch? If someone doesn't bring her to me immediately, I will murder every last one of you."

"Whoa there, Zane," Cooper says while holding his hands up. "Calm down. We all want to help you, but that witch has unbelievable powers. She skedaddled after you did. Before she left, she threatened everyone in town, telling 'em she'd eevis, eeviz, ah... Lucy, you remember what Kezia said?"

"Sure 'nuff. That witch said she'd eviscerate everybody."

Lucy spoke the word eviscerate with great care, as if she had never needed to pronounce it before. Well, I doubt a saloon owner has any need for such terms.

The wench hugs herself and winces, as if in anticipation of a lashing. "Can't ya just, um, use your powers to bring Kezia here? I mean, Zor'imuth could do that. You're his son."

But my powers were diminished by the usurper Rahn'omith and by the sorceress. Rahn did that solely to punish me for being the son of Zor'imuth. I have no idea why Mazdala wanted to kill me. Maybe Rahn forced her to do it.

I need those fucking powers back. Now.

Lucy sidles up to me, rubbing her body against mine even while she continues to cringe faintly. "Don't mean to make ya spittin' mad again. But I've always heard that demons can gain power from, ya know, hanky-panky."

I grunt. "Suddenly a whore can't speak the word fuck. This truly is an alternate reality."

"Well, do ya want my help or not?"

My body hungers for Charlotte Fortescue, but I need more power if I ever want to achieve my goal. To destroy the wolf and his mate, I must first destroy their beloved daughter. That means I need to strengthen my magics. "Yes, Lucy, today is your lucky day. A demon is going to fuck you."

CHAPTER SIX

Charlotte

BY THE TIME I RETURN TO WILDERHAMPTON, I CAN'T REMEMBER why I ever thought Zane was intriguing. Honestly, the man behaved bizarrely the entire time. I might have gotten slightly aroused when he touched me, but he ruined any chance he had of getting under my skirts when he snarled at me. I swear he sounded like a wolf then. But he can't be a werewolf. Can he? Even my parents wouldn't know the answer to that question. Well, maybe Dad could sniff out a wolf since he used to be one.

No more thinking about Zane. It's time for bed.

Surprisingly, I fall asleep within minutes of laying my head down on the pillow. I dream of strange events and strange creatures, red-skinned beings who have huge, rippling muscles and devour meat raw as the blood of their prey dribbles down their chins. They grunt and growl and stamp their feet. Then a creature saunters into the rock-hewn chamber, and the others freeze, clearly afraid of the newcomer.

The one they fear is Zane. He is a red-skinned being like the others.

He swivels his head toward me, as if I'm an invisible observer in this nightmare. "Charlotte, daughter of the wolf, you will be mine. When I come to you again, I will whisper sinful things in your ear, and you will give your-self to me willingly, body and soul. Your ecstasy will feed my hunger."

My lids fly open. My heart pounds, and a cold sweat dampens my satin chemise. I sit up, holding a hand over my heart, and wait for the panic to subside. Never in my life have I dreamed about such vile, evil creatures. Some-how I know that if I met those beings in real life, they would ravage me in every possible manner, and I would end up dead.

But it was only a dream. Yes, only a dream.

Once my pulse has returned to normal, I go into the loo to splash cool water on my face. Fortunately, my suite includes an attached bathroom. That means I don't need to worry about bumping into Mum or Dad and having to ex-plain why I seem so frazzled.

My chemise is clammy now, thanks to that cold sweat. Though I could rummage through my dresser for an old nightdress, I decide to sleep in the nude for the rest of the night. I'm too knackered to search for some-thing else, and I would need to turn on the lamp to do that. Mum and Dad would surely notice the glow com-ing from my door.

I slide under the covers and pull them up to my chin, then roll onto my side. Soon, I drift into slumber once again.

Warm, rough hands glide over my belly. The sensa-tion of those calluses on my skin arouses me, and I moan softly. The hard body molded to my backside feels delicious pressed against me, and I moan again, more loudly, when a stiff cock brushes against my arse.

"Charlotte, sweet Charlotte, I will revel in debauching you."

"Zane?" I say, too sleepy to understand what's happening in this dream.

"Yes, it's me." He slides a hand between my thighs, lift-ing one leg so he can push his long, stiff, throbbing cock be-tween my folds. "I could smell your lust for me the moment I entered this bedchamber. You want me, and I will make you come so many times that you'll barely be able to speak, much less walk."

"Mm, that sounds lovely." Why shouldn't I indulge in this dirty dream? It feels too bloody good, and I'm not ready to wake up yet.

His callused finger rubs my clitoris. "I won't fuck you, not yet. But after tonight, you'll beg me to come to you again and take your body, pleasuring you in the filthiest manner."

"Oh, yes, please."

"For tonight, this is what I'll give you. An appetizer."

He glides his hand up and down my cleft, teasing my nub every time the heel of his hand brushes against it. I can't stop myself. I begin to rock my hips into his palm, then I bend my knee to give him more leverage. My wetness trickles down my thighs while he groans and shoves a hand under me to grasp my breast and massage the nipple until I cry out. I fist my hands in the pillow. He growls, then seals his lips to mine.

The second he slips his tongue into my mouth, I melt for him.

Zane kisses me so tenderly but with a raw sensuality that takes my breath away. No one has ever made love to my mouth like this. I should break the kiss, but I don't want to. The scent of him surrounds me, an indescribable aroma that turns me on even more strongly. I writhe and try to roll onto my back, desperate to take him inside me, hungry for all the sensual fire he can give me.

Then Zane rises to his knees.

I can't rip my focus away from his nude body. His cock is enormous and so stiff that it could probably break a steel bar. He clasps his erection and pumps it casually as if he has all the time in the world to spend with me, here in this room. "You aren't ready yet, Charlotte. Next time you beg me to fuck you, I won't be so gentle. But you'll beg me to ravage you, and you'll come so hard your eyes will roll back in your head."

"Don't leave, please. I'm loving this dream."

He chuckles darkly. "Dream? If you believe that, you'll have a rude awakening in the morning."

Zane pumps his cock faster, tipping his head back to groan with deep pleasure. Beads of moisture glisten on the crown. The moonlight filtering in through the windows accentuates those drops, and my mouth waters, afflicting me with a thirst for licking his flesh clean. But I can't move or do anything but gawp at him. He speeds up his movements, bending over me to grasp the headboard with his other hand. Now that he hovers above me, he abruptly freezes.

"You're going to do this for me, little Charlotte. Take my cock in your hand, then pump until I come all over your sweet little body."

I might as well finish this dream and do what he tells me. I'm so desperate for an orgasm that I can't think anymore. All I can do is take hold of his engorged cock and slide my hand up and down, up and down, moving faster and faster while he hisses in a sharp breath and begins to thrust into the movements of my hands.

Zane snarls and shouts.

And he comes all over my belly. The jet of his release feels hot and smells like the most sinful dessert on earth. I keep stroking him until the last drops are gone.

He touches my lips with one finger. "Hush, my little pet, and go to sleep. Tomorrow night, I'll give you what you want more than anything—me inside you."

My lids flutter shut.

The next thing I know, I'm waking up with sunshine pouring in the through the balcony doors, which hang open. What? No, I didn't leave the doors open. Did I? *Bloody hell*. I've become a sleepwalker or...something. But when I sit up, cold floods through me.

Because my belly is covered with a milky substance.

Oh, no, no, no. I leap off the bed and race into the bathroom. No, no, it was a dream, that's all. I didn't let a strange man touch me intimately and spill his nocturnal emissions all over me. No, I would never beg Zane to shag me. Only in a fantasy might I ever consider doing anything so insane. Since I hadn't climaxed in the dream, that means it was only a nightmare.

Oh, yes, because nightmares are often salacious and pleasurable.

I jump into the shower and frantically scrub away the remnants of what Zane had deposited on my belly, almost as if it were a brand. How did Zane even get into my room? So much for Wilderhampton's high-tech security.

After my shower, I shuffle to the balcony doors and lean forward to glance around the area. There are no trellises that might let someone climb into my bedroom. I can't imagine how Zane could have sneaked into my room.

Somehow, I manage to behave normally when I go downstairs for breakfast. Mum and Dad are already seated at the table, chatting and laughing. I feel like rubbish, like I've joined the dark side and now I'll be condemned to eternity in hell for my crimes, like Persephone in Greek mythology. But I didn't eat any pomegranates. My parents don't seem to have noticed anything odd about me this morning, thank goodness. Under no circumstances will I confess to anyone that a stranger I met yesterday crept into my room overnight and teased me with his mouth, his hands, and his cock.

It must've been a dream. Nothing else makes sense.

Maybe I could convince myself of that if I hadn't woken up with a stark reminder of Zane's presence plastered all over my belly.

The worst part is that I loved the way he touched me.

"Are you all right, Charlotte?" Mum asks. "You don't seem like yourself this morning."

My attempt to behave normally didn't work, did it? Of course not. "I'm fine, Mum. Just a little tired."

Dad scrutinizes me. "Did your students exhaust you, pet?"

"No. I love my students." But I need to come up with some sort of excuse for how tired I am. "I think the commute is getting to me lately."

Mum clasps my hand. "Why don't you find a flat to lease closer to the school?"

"I love living here at Wilderhampton."

What if Zane comes back tonight? He might make me come so hard that I scream. No, he won't do that because I will never let him. He knows I live here at Wilderhampton, though I have no bloody idea how he found that out since I never told him my surname or where I live.

"Sweetie, we know you love it here," Mum says. "But I don't like seeing you so wiped out. Maybe just for the rest of this week you could stay in a hotel. Your dad and I will pay for it."

"I can afford to pay for my own hotel." Zane won't find me there. Probably. In a naughty little corner of my mind, I wish he would slink into my room again. But I do not allow my subconscious desires to take control. Well, not anymore. The Zane incident was an anomaly. "Yes, I think I will try a hotel. Just for this week."

Mum squeezes my hand. "I'm so glad, sweetie."

Dad smiles at Mum and sighs. "You're hoping our daughter will meet a respectable young man and fall in love. Aren't you, Kylie?"

"Possibly. What's wrong with that?"

"Nothing, love." He winks at me. "Go, have your fun. If you return with a boyfriend, your mother will throw a huge do to celebrate."

Mum pretends to scowl at him. "No, I won't, Nathaniel."

I clear my throat. "Now that we've settled that, I'll go pack a bag and be on my way."

"Call us every evening, okay? Your father will be heart-broken if you don't."

Dad rolls his gaze heavenward and shakes his head. "Why do I put up with women? You're all barmy."

Mum kisses his cheek. "You love us, that's why."

Fifteen minutes later, I'm in my car driving to the school. The day rushes by, and before I know it, I'm check-ing in at a hotel in Chelsea. Why did I choose this district? It's the closest place where I can find a hotel that isn't too far from the school. It has nothing to do with Zane.

Sometimes I feel guilty for having a very generous al-lowance. But tonight, I don't worry about that at all. I've had a very strange week so far, and I deserve a beautiful hotel room that has a jacuzzi in the loo and a bed large enough to fit a whole cricket team. All right, that could be a slight ex-aggeration. But this bed is enormous.

Just like Zane.

No, I will not think about *him* anymore.

I don't have a balcony, but I do have a huge picture win-dow in the living room. After ordering a meal with dessert and consuming all of it in five minutes, I change into my satin chemise. Then, I approach the big window and gaze out at the lights of the city.

A pair of arms, the muscular sort, slides around my waist. "Don't want Mommy and Daddy to hear us fucking tonight, eh?"

My breath catches. A thrill zings through me.

I turn my head to see Zane's face. "How did you get in here?"

"Magic, sweet Charlotte, magic."

"Are you a werewolf?"

He smiles with devilish delight and nods toward the window. "Tonight is the full moon. If I were a wolf, I'd be licking your ankles right now."

"Oh, yes. That does make sense." My behavior doesn't make sense, though. I should feel guilty for what happened last night, and I absolutely should not let Zane touch me again. He hasn't even explained his mysterious appearance. Magic? That's bollocks. "You must have bribed the bellboy to let you in here."

"I have no need of doors or bellboys. If I want you, I will find you anywhere. There will be nothing you can do to stop me."

"Rubbish." I try to wriggle out of his embrace, but he has me pinned to his body, firmly yet not painfully. "Please let go of me. I do not want to have sex with you."

He nuzzles the top of my head. "You smell sinfully good. If you aren't a bad girl, why did you let me touch you last night? And why have you been waiting for me to come to you again?"

"I wasn't waiting. I was enjoying the view."

Zane captures my earlobe and suckles it gently, making me gasp. "I bet you had never been as wet for any man as you were for me last night."

Enough of this. I need to get away from Zane before my traitorous body melts for him. So, I stomp my foot down on his arch. He doesn't even grunt or lose his hold on me. I slam my elbow backward, but his taut muscles cause me pain while he seems unaffected. Does he have steel cables under his skin?

Zane glides his hands up to my breasts, cupping them. When he flicks a finger across my nipple, I gasp again. And he chuckles. "See? You can't hide your lust for me. The good girl wants to go bad."

"No, I do not want that."

"Of course you do. The scent of your desire is driving me mad."

"Brilliant. I hope you do go mad. Then I'll have the advantage."

A strange sensation of...something ripples through the room. It had a palpable effect, like a wave of heat rising off concrete on a sweltering summer day. The view of the city ripples too.

"What are you doing, Zane?"

"Nothing." He pulls away from me and staggers toward the window. "This is—not—me."

I hurry backwards as the shimmering ripple expands and warps not only the view beyond the window but also the air inside this hotel suite. "What's going on? Feels like the room is pressurized. Getting hard to...breathe."

Zane's chest heaves as if he can hardly breathe either. He whirls around and rushes toward me, holding me to his body as if he's protecting me. From what?

We're about to find out.

CHAPTER SEVEN

Zane

I WRAP MY ARMS AROUND CHARLOTTE AS IF THAT WILL SHIELD HER from whatever magics are being invoked here. Why someone wants to do this, I can't explain. Who has done it... I have my suspicions about that. But why the Rom witch would wish to create ripples of supernatural energy within this room remains a mystery.

The walls begin to shudder. The floor beneath our feet trembles too. The tremors grow stronger every second.

"Kezia!" I shout. "Stop this and show yourself."

Charlotte cranes her neck to glimpse the chaos unfolding around us. She is brave, for certain. Anyone else would likely run away. But she remains here, not frozen in fear, but wary and full of curiosity. She is an unusual woman. But then, it shouldn't surprise me that the daughter of a werewolf would possess an iron strength of will.

"Kezia! I command you to stop."

Cackling erupts from nowhere in particular, seeming to emanate from every corner of the room all at once.

The simmering magics abruptly cease.

Charlotte wriggles out of my grasp. This time, I let her do it. I have more pressing issues to deal with, such as the Rom witch who stands before the floor-to-ceiling window. Her hair rises off her shoulders to swirl around her head. But it's the red and black glistening in her irises that give me pause.

Kezia jabs a finger toward me. "You will be punished for your sins, Zaen'imuth, son of Zor'imuth."

"I had never met you until yesterday. I have done nothing to you."

"Lies! Every word is a falsehood spilling from your wicked lips."

Cautiously, I take two steps toward her. "What do you claim I have done?"

She spreads her arms, and another ripple rushes over me, stealing my breath. "You must suffer for the sins of your father. You are just like him. Zor'imuth destroyed my family when he took Erosabel as his mistress, against her will. Zor'imuth was but a princeling, yet he had dreams of conquering the human world. The demon destroyed so many of the Rom and all the Kevitash. Now you must pay for those atrocities."

"No, Kezia. You are the one who will die tonight."

I rush at her faster than any human could move and clamp my hands around her throat. But as I squeeze, she cackles. With a flick of one finger, she sends me hurtling backward. I slam down on my backside. Charlotte just managed to scurry out of the way before my body could crush her.

Kezia spreads her arms once again, tips her head back, and shouts in a language I don't understand. Finally, she relaxes. Her gaze lands on me, and her lips curve into a wicked smile. "It is done."

I leap to my feet. "What is done?"

She cackles again.

And I barrel toward her.

Kezia vanishes.

I smack into the window. For a moment, I'm too stunned to move. Then I slowly peel myself away from the glass and turn around to face Charlotte. She stands on the other side of the room, her eyes wide. Before I can open my mouth to speak, the room begins to whirl and tilt around us while a violent gale swirls through the whole room. The power of the wind escalates every second, until it becomes too strong to fight. All I can do is stand in this spot and grit my teeth.

Charlotte stumbles toward me, flailing for a foothold, but it's too late.

A force beyond comprehension sucks us into oblivion.

I'm thrown into a whirlwind. The sheer power of it lashes me like a hundred whips cracking into my flesh, and the taste of blood fills my mouth. Then, as quickly as the tempest began, it ends. An eerie silence echoes around me. I stagger sideways as my senses struggle to sort out my surroundings. I blink several times until, at last, my vision and my hearing return to normal.

And I fist my hands. This is the Outlands. That blasted witch threw me into this pocket realm. Why? She knows this region belongs to the demon hordes.

I glance around but can't see Charlotte anywhere—or the Rom witch. Where are the residents of this cursed town? Even the buildings appear dark and empty. Of course, the residents might have shut off all the lights to hide from me. That will not work.

A faint figure shimmers before me, then resolves into a specific being.

I lunge for Kezia, intending to snap her neck, but my fists bounce off her. A protective spell, I'm sure. She knows I will be furious and she will die if I can lay even one finger on her.

"What are you doing, Kezia? Where have you sent Charlotte?"

The witch sneers at me. "Thus begins your punishment. You will suffer until the day you beg me to destroy you."

I grit my teeth and snarl, "What have you done, witch?"

Kezia sneers again with all the lustful anger of a hell beast. "I summoned all the powers of the Rom and the Kevitash to mete out Zor'imuth's punishment through you, Zaen'imuth. You will never again leave the Outlands—unless you can miraculously change your evil ways. That seems unlikely."

"This cannot be the Outlands. It's too clean."

"Once I am gone, the merging will begin." She raises her arms high above her head. "Let it all be done."

A pulse of energy slams into me, knocking me off balance, then evaporates. Lights flare to life inside the buildings, and I can see figures moving around within the structures. But the lights appear to be a combination of modern electric lighting as well as candles and oil lamps.

"Where is this place?"

"I've told you this is the Outlands. The new version of it." She sneers at me. "You should have asked when this is. Alas, it's too late now."

Kezia disappears.

Lucy and Cooper trot out of the saloon, halting before me. The saloon whore speaks first. "What happened to you, hon? Don't look so good. Somebody gave you a towelling, huh?"

"I don't understand your words." I had learned modern English to help me seduce Charlotte, but Wild West language still confounds me. "Where is Charlotte?"

Lucy shrugs. "Don't know what she looks like."

"She has dark hair, hazel eyes that are almost blue-gray, and porcelain skin."

"Ain't seen nobody like that."

The sound of a scuffle erupts from further down the street. A woman's voice shouts words I can't quite hear. I run toward the ruckus faster than any human could accomplish the feat and seize the throat of the bedraggled man who dared to grab Charlotte's arm. "Release her now."

The demonic tone of my voice seems to convince the cretin. He raises his hands. "Sorry, I was just bein' friendly."

"What is your name?"

"Ezra."

I shake him so hard that his head snaps backward. "I am the sheriff. That means I own this town. If you ever touch this woman again, I will rip your guts out of your belly and stuff them down your throat."

The second I release my hold on him, he shuffles backward several paces. "I-I won't never even look at her, I swear it."

I wave him away. "Be gone from my sight."

Ezra sprints down the street.

Charlotte gapes at me, her jaw slack.

"Did that savage harm you?" I ask. "He must have done something to you since you're incapable of speech."

"I can speak. But you..." She shakes her head slowly. "Is this the real you?"

"What else can I be but the real me? You must have hit your head on a hard object, and it's left you dazed."

She swallows hard enough that I can see the movement in her throat. "What are you, Zane?"

I bow my head to study my own body. A low growl emerges from me. Kezia has exposed my true nature. I am once again a monstrous demon with skin that glistens a golden red shade. My eyes must look darker and more demonic as well. That Rom witch will suffer for eternity once I escape from this place and hunt her down.

Charlotte's initial shock seems to have faded.

I rotate in a circle to survey the area. "This is the Outlands, but also something else. I don't know what it is."

"This is Wrathrock."

"What is Wrathrock? I have never heard of such a domain."

Charlotte moves closer. "It's an Old West ghost town, a tourist attraction, in the middle of the Utah desert."

"But we are not in the mortal world." I rub my jaw, remembering what Kezia had told me. "The Rom witch said that once she was gone, the merging would begin. She must have meant that the past and present of the Outlands would become one."

"Can't you send me back to England? I have nothing to do with any of this."

I bend over to align our gazes. "You have everything to do with this."

"Rubbish. I don't even know who or what you really are, and you don't know me either."

"That might be true, but it changes nothing that I've said. You are the central element of my plan."

She sets her hands on her hips. "Why me? I am a stranger to you."

A deep, dark chuckle rumbles out of me. "After that night in your bedroom, we aren't strangers anymore, sweet Charlotte."

"Stop calling me 'sweet.' I'm not your pet." She maintains her defiant stance, even while I can see her lips trembling the slightest bit. "Tell me why you're doing this to me. I deserve an explanation. Please."

Oh, yes, she spoke the word please as if the taste of it sours her tongue.

I will explain my motivations to her, strictly to ensure she understands the stakes and will obey me. But I won't share that information with her out here on the street with all these miscreants hovering nearby. That leaves me with one alternative.

I seize Charlotte and hoist her into my arms, then stalk toward the saloon. Naturally, she can't stop herself from harassing me. The girl assures me that I will "regret messing with the daughter of an earl" and that she will rip my "bollocks" off if I try to force myself on her. She also kicks her legs repeatedly and bites my hand. None of that bothers me. She might as well be swatting flies for all the good it does her.

Lucy and Cooper follow us, but I don't care about that.

The interior of the saloon has remained essentially the same, despite the merging of the Wild West with certain aspects of the twenty-first century. Good. I need access to the room where Nathaniel Fortescue had once imprisoned Kylie, the woman who would eventually become his wife.

I take the stairs four at a time and kick the bedroom door open. Then, I toss Charlotte onto the bed. She bounces on the mattress, just like her tits bounce on her chest. She winds up sprawled on the bed with her chemise half off one shoulder. A low growl escapes my lips. To see almost all of one breast ignites my lust. Right now, it's a low simmer. That won't last long, though. Soon, I will need to fuck her.

Lucy and Cooper rush into the room.

The wench speaks up first. "If you're needing us to guard your new thang, honey, just let us know. Cooper can keep watch while I look after your piece of calico."

My what? I've never heard such a phrase before, but I am in the Wild West—the Outlands version. I will hear many strange phrases. I've also never heard anyone refer to a woman as a "thang."

"Leave us," I snarl. "Both of you, be gone."

Lucy and Cooper scurry away, shutting the door behind them.

And I stalk up to Charlotte, bending over her. "You belong to me. And I am about to explain why."

She squints at my chest, where my shirt had been partially torn open during our journey into the Outlands. "I thought a demon would have bright red skin. But yours is only slightly red, with golden undertones. Your complexion might be lovely if you weren't such an arsehole."

I bend further toward her and hiss, "Be silent, woman."

"Be silent yourself, asshat."

My brows draw together. "Asshat?"

"Yeah, that's what my mum calls a man who's a complete and total wanker. She even called my father an asshat when they first met."

Her words do not clear up the "asshat" issue. But that's irrelevant. "If you don't stop speaking, I will ravish you right here, right now, with no regard for what sort of condition I'll leave you in."

Charlotte huffs. "I am not afraid of you." She reaches out to touch my forehead and cautiously explore my scalp. "Why don't you have horns? I thought Satan had those, and so do the demons in mythology and religion."

"Be quiet, or I'll—"

"Do what? Growl at me? Please. You aren't that frightening." She wriggles backward on the bed just enough that she can sit up without brushing my chest. "Tell me your grand plan and get it over with."

I notice a chair in the corner by the bed and drag it closer to Charlotte, dropping onto the seat with a thunk. Now, I can keep my eye on the girl while I explain. "My father removed my horns because he despised me. But your mother murdered him. I am the son of Zor'imuth, the former king of the demon hordes. Kylie Drummond tricked him and then destroyed him. Nathaniel Fortescue helped her."

Charlotte rolls her eyes. "Your father was an evil fiend."

I slide forward in my chair, planting my hands at either side of her hips. "I intend to seek revenge for the slaying of my father. And you are the tool I will use to enact my vengeance."

"You loved your father very much, I assume."

"I despised him as much as he despised me."

She makes an odd face that twists her features. "If you hated him, why bother avenging his death?"

"Because he was my father."

Charlotte seems unaffected by my disdainful tone. "That doesn't make sense. And even if your demented plan were reasonable, kidnapping me won't get you what you want."

"Of course it will." I grasp her chin, leaning in until my lips hover a hair's breadth from hers. "I will defile you in every way imaginable. Not only your body will be ruined, but your mind and your soul will be too. When I return you to your parents, they won't recognize you anymore—and you will beg me to take you back to my lair."

She huffs again. "My parents aren't that stupid. They'll know something hinky happened, and they will never believe that I would willingly go with a demon."

"Remember the other night? I came to you in your room, and your parents never knew what happened. I'd wager you never even told them I'd visited you." I scrape my thumb across her lip. "Because you wanted me to pleasure you again tonight. I'll give you what you want as soon as you give yourself to me willingly."

"That will never happen. *You* will have to beg *me* to shag you." She puckers her lips. "And I'll tell you to sod off."

I delicately trace my tongue over her bottom lip, making her shiver just enough that I know I've got her. "You will dream of me, sweet Charlotte. And when you awaken, you'll beg me to fuck you."

While she glowers at me, I stalk out the door and slam it behind me.

CHAPTER EIGHT

Charlotte

THAT BLOODY DEMON. HE THINKS HE'S A GENIUS AT SEDUCING WOMEN, but the only thing he arouses in me is anger. Maybe I did dream of him and have an orgasm because of the erotic nature of my fantasy, but Zane will never touch me that intimately in real life. If he turns up in my dreams tonight, I'll punch him in the gut. Better yet, I'll find a hard metal object and whack him over the head with it.

Who am I kidding? That dream was not normal. I know Zane was in the room with me. Ever since I found out what he really is, I'm convinced that he used spells to make me want him. But I have a secret weapon, one that he failed to notice. I had tucked it inside my chemise, hanging low enough that even its chain is difficult to see.

The Kevitash medallion hangs low between my breasts.

I should have thrust it into Zane's face, but I'd been too confused by the witch's arrival and her bizarre threats. The next time I see Zane, I'll mash the medallion to his face and let it burn off every millimeter of his demonic skin. After all, when Mum first met Dad, he stole the medallion from her, and it scorched his flesh. It must do the same for a demon.

But I feel weird about doing that. Maybe it's because he confessed that his own father removed his devil horns. I wanted to question him about how that happened and why, as well as how it made him feel. I'm sure a demon male will be no less reticent about discussing his feelings than a human man would be. A demon might be even more stubborn.

His feelings don't matter to me. I need to escape. That is my only goal.

Fortunately, this is the same room where Dad imprisoned Mum when she annoyed him with her snarky comments and willful determination. When I turned sixteen, my parents had decided I was old enough to know the whole story of how they fell in love and conceived me. Mum loves to tell and retell the tale of what went on between them in this room. It has great significance to them both. I learned a lot about this place before I ever met a certain demon.

For one, I know the walls are ironclad. The windows have iron bars too.

As I stare at the door and rack my brain for a solution to my problem, a simple fact suddenly occurs to me. That bloody demon forgot to lock the door. I would've heard a noise, a "chunk" or something, that would've alerted me to the fact he'd trapped me in here—if he had done that. But I didn't hear a chunk or a clunk. He was fuming when he left, and I rather doubt he was thinking clearly enough to remember to secure the ironclad room.

All right, then. I have a chance to escape.

While wearing nothing but a thin satin chemise that barely covers my arse. Oh, yes, I'd love to jog downstairs to the saloon where men will lick their chops at the chance to assault me. *Screw that.* I need clothes. I'll get out of here first, running past those slavering degenerates faster than their drunken brains can comprehend what's happening.

I am the daughter of a wolf and a demon killer, after all.

As I approach the door, I rest my hand on the cold metal of the knob. The hesitation lasts for only a second or two. Then I cautiously open the door and step out into the hall. I can hear the saloon customers talking rather loudly, and I also hear Lucy too. Her laughter is unmistakable, like a cross between a cackling witch and a bawdy singer.

I will only get one chance to escape. Can I run past those cretins without getting caught? Could there be another option? I study the hallway and its multiple doors. Maybe I should try one of those. Back when Mum and Dad were here, only the one room had been ironclad. Might as well try the others before I brave the gauntlet downstairs.

As I tiptoe down the hall, someone starts playing a piano down in the saloon. Then, several people begin to sing a bawdy drinking song. That's the perfect cover for me. I stop at the first door and cautiously try to turn the knob. No luck. It's locked. I move on to the next door, trying that one too, but I have no better luck. Who knew Wild West cretins were so security conscious? I have two more doors to try, so I move on to the next one and gently try to turn it.

Eureka. It's unlocked.

I twist the knob as quietly as possible and slip inside the room, shutting the door gently. Then I survey the cramped space, which has only a small bed and one chair plus a tiny dresser. A man's clothing lies strewn over the floor and the furniture. I tiptoe around all of that, reaching the window—which has no bars on it. *Hallelujah.* But when I grip the bottom edge and try to lift the window, the sash won't move. I think the sill has been painted over onto the window frame. I need something to scrape it off with, but all I have is the medallion.

Well, why can't I use that? It's made of metal.

I pull out the medallion and use its sharp edge to do just that, managing to scrape off enough paint to free the window. But I struggle to hoist the sash. Then it pops open abruptly, making a noise that I doubt—or perhaps hope—the drunkards downstairs won't have heard. I set my hands on the sill and lean forward to assess the situation below me. I'm on the second floor, but I already knew that. Directly beneath me, I see...nothing. Just hard earth.

Maybe I'll get bruised if I jump, but I don't care.

I throw one leg over the sill, now balanced over it, and take two quick, deep breaths. Then, I leap out the window.

My bare feet whump down on the hard earth. I lose my balance and bump into the building. But I won't wait to find out if anyone heard that or saw me leaping out the window. I race behind the saloon and run out across the desert toward a destination I've seen only once before, yet I know precisely where to go. I pray the Kevitash butte will grant me entry into its passageway and lead me to the chamber where Mum and Dad had once hidden.

I run, run, run, faster than I ever imagined I could. Rocks cut my soles, but I don't give a toss about that. Get to the butte, that's all I can think of.

A hulking shape appears in front of me.

Zane lashes his arms around me. "Did you think it would be that easy, sweet Charlotte? Not as clever as you think you are, eh?"

Bloody hell. I struggle against his hold on me and even bite him, but he only chuckles. "Let me go, you disgusting brute. I will never shag you. Never. I'll kill myself first."

He springs into the air while still holding on to me, soaring upward so high that I can barely see the town below us. The demon drops back down onto the dusty street right in front of the saloon. "You cannot get away from me. Make things easier for yourself and give in. I promise when we fuck, you will experience ecstasy like nothing any human male could show you."

"I don't give a damn about ecstasy. I want freedom."

Lucy and Cooper race out of the saloon, halting near us. Lucy sneers at me. "You don't need this little thang, Zane. I gave you all the power you needed when we done it like rabbits in heat. Get rid of this little girl and let me serve you in any way you like."

Zane releases me so abruptly that I stumble sideways. He grasps Lucy's throat with one huge hand, squeezing hard enough to make her gurgle. "Never again speak to me about Charlotte or suggest I should fuck you. That was once and never again." He hurls Lucy away, sending her flying backward. "From this moment forward, if you wish to stay alive, you will speak to me only if I ask you to. Understood?"

Lucy's lips tremble, and her eyes bulge. "Yeah, I understand. Please forgive me, Zane."

"You will call me 'master.' "

She scrambles to her feet, visibly shaking from head to toe. "Please forgive me, master."

Lucy scurries back inside the saloon.

Cooper bites his lip, his brows furrowed. "Why'd ya do that to poor Lucy? I ain't criticizing, just confused."

And scared, though he won't say so.

Zane glowers at him. "Do you want to be confined in the bottom of a well? If not, then turn around and go back into the saloon."

The nasty tone of his voice makes me shiver faintly. Cooper is visibly shaken—and shaking. The poor boy races into the saloon.

I round on Zane. "Why did you terrify those two? They've been on your side, almost worshiping you, though I can't figure out why. Behaving like a bully will not gain you any friends."

"Why should I care about befriending these wretches?" He seizes my arm, dragging me closer. "You still have no idea what sort of place this is, do you? Sweet little Charlotte is oblivious of what's right in front of her."

"You're in quite a foul mood. It doesn't suit you."

He laughs, though it's not a cheerful sound. "You know nothing about me except that I fucked Lucy moments before I found you again. And yet, you still want to ride my cock."

"Don't be so crude."

"Why not? My crudeness makes you wet." Despite everyone watching us, he shoves his hand inside my chemise and palms my breast, roughly flicking his fingernaile over the nipple and making me gasp. Then he lowers his head to within millimeters of mine. "You're a dirty girl underneath all that prim attitude. The daughter of a werewolf could never be a good girl. Give in to your animal nature and revel in the pleasure I'll give you. It will be filthy, and you'll beg me to do whatever I want to you."

"Oh, you arrogant, rude, foul-mouthed blighter. I'd shag a tree before I'd get naked with you."

But I am wet, and that fact disturbs me. I let him touch me intimately the other night, and just thinking about it makes my clitoris throb.

He stares at my lips as if he means to devour them, too distracted to notice what I'm doing.

I reach inside my chemise to pull out the medallion and crush it to his bare chest.

Zane clutches the medallion, attempting to tear it away from his flesh, but the metal liquifies his skin. Drops of his molten flesh hit the ground and sizzle. The demon roars as he staggers backward, snapping the chain, clutching at the medallion as blood pours from his chest. Despite the chain flapping, the medallion sinks deeper and deeper into Zane's flesh. The agony on his face and in his voice tugs at something deep inside me as if my conscience is pricking at me for what I've done. Why should I care if he dies? The demon has vowed to do vicious, depraved things to me.

Yet he hasn't followed through on any of those threats.

I can't fight the impulse any longer, so I fall to my knees beside him. His eyes are bulging as if they might pop out of his skull. He gurgles and gasps as if he can't breathe. How can I save him? Why I want to spare him is an issue I'll wrestle with later. For now, I do the only thing I can think to try. The medallion is embedded deep in his flesh now, and I need to push my fingers in there to feel around until I locate the metal disk.

Zane jerks and cries out.

Wincing, I try not to look at his agonized face while I dig my fingers even deeper into his body to grasp the medallion. Then I carefully pull it free of his rotting flesh. He howls, and his face has gone pale, masking his red skin tone. I remove the medallion and set it on the ground. Zane looks half dead already. His eyes are shut, his breathing has grown dangerously shallow, and blood streams from his open wound. The scarlet liquid begins to pool around us both.

"Someone help me!" I shout. "Is there a doctor in this godforsaken town? Please, someone do something."

Cooper shuffles over to us, though I hadn't noticed when he reappeared. "He's too dang big, miss. I can't carry him alone."

I rise to my feet. "If you lot don't help me save him, I will destroy every last one of you." I hold up the medallion. "This is my magic. You've seen what I can do, so help me or die!"

Will I actually kill anyone? I can't answer that question with any degree of certainty, not anymore.

Cooper spins around and races to the saloon, flinging the doors open. "Ezra! Jasper! Hank! Get your damn asses out here."

The other three men hesitate only for a few seconds. Then they sprint out of the saloon and follow Cooper over to where Zane lies bleeding. Cooper recruits them to assist with lifting Zane. The demon is not only enormous but also much heavier than a human of his size would be. I follow the men as they heave Zane off the ground and carry him with two men on each side of the demon.

Lucy emerges from the saloon. Her eyes fly wide.

"Where are we taking Zane?" I demand. "He needs a doctor."

She makes a rude noise. "Doctor? This is the Outlands, missy. We ain't got no medical types here."

I notice a good number of people have gathered along the periphery of the street, sticking close to the buildings as they watch the drama unfolding out here. "If any of you have medical training, get your sodding arses over here and come with us." I hold up the medallion. "Don't test my patience!"

No one would ever have called me dangerous or even mildly threatening, not in all my life before this moment. Coming to the Outlands and meeting Zane has changed me, but I don't have time to consider the consequences.

A man separates from the crowd, near the porch of the sheriff's office. A woman seizes his arm as if she means to stop him. He pats her hand, then jogs across the street to join our little procession.

"I'm Robert Hooper," he tells me. "I'm an anesthesiologist. I should be able to do something for that, uh, gentleman."

He winced when he called Zane a gentleman.

I study Robert Hooper for a few seconds. "You don't seem like the sort who would wind up in the Outlands."

"The what lands? Never heard of it."

"How did you come to be here in this town?"

"My wife and I saw a road sign advertising Wrathrock Ghost Town and thought it sounded like fun. And it was a hoot—until everything changed." He glances at the buildings and the strange denizens of the Outlands. "We got swept up in some kind of... I don't know. It was almost like a tornado."

"You are in the Outlands now, though I prefer to call this place Wrathrock. It's where the wicked come to live out eternity, or at least that's what I believe it is. You and several other tourists got caught up in whatever's happening here."

We've just arrived at the saloon doors. Lucy and I swing them open so the men can carry Zane inside. They manage to drag him up the stairs to the second floor. When Cooper asks where we should leave the demon, I wave toward the ironclad room. Can't think of anywhere else to put him. Once the men have deposited Zane on the bed, most of them leave. Only Cooper and Robert remain.

Robert stares down at the demon, his brows furrowed. "What is this guy?"

"He is the demon Zaen'imuth. But he prefers to be called Zane."

"Demon?" Robert goes a touch pale but squares his shoulders and performs a quick visual inspection of his patient. "Well, guess I better get to work. Don't suppose you have any medical instruments."

I glance at Cooper, who shrugs. "Apparently not. Do your best, that's all I'm asking."

"Sure. I'll give it the old college try."

Zane moans.

I sit on the bed beside him, clasping his big red hand. And I pray for a demon to live.

CHAPTER NINE

Zane

ROBERT AND COOPER BOTH SEEM MYSTIFIED BY CHARLOTTE'S BEHAV-ior. I'm equally confused by her need to save me. Why should she care if I disintegrate into a million broken molecules? I've been nothing but cruel to her, deceiving the girl about my true nature and tricking her into letting me touch her intimately. I can't comprehend why Charlotte is desperately trying to comfort me, or why she wants to keep me alive.

The doctor, Robert, sighs and sets about examining his patient. I know this because I've suddenly found that I have the strength to open my eyes, if only a sliver.

"Charlotte," I croak.

"I'm here."

"Are you...injured?"

"Me? No. You're the one who has a bloody great hole in your chest."

I attempt to lift my head, but it falls back down, seeming to weigh a thousand pounds. "The medallion..."

"Yes, I know. It's what caused your injuries. I'm sorry, Zane. I never meant for you to die."

Before I can point out all the reasons why she should let me die, my lids drift shut and my head falls to the side. But I can still hear everything going on around me. I'm unable to speak, so naturally, everyone in the room will assume I'm unconscious.

"Don't worry," Robert says. "He's still alive. But I'm not sure how to stop the bleeding. Could you grab some towels? Maybe I can stanch the flow that way."

"I can get those," Cooper says. "Lucy has towels behind the bar for wiping up."

Cooper races out of the room, which I know because I hear his footfalls pounding down the staircase. Only a moment passes before he clomps upstairs again. He must have left the door to this room open. "Here are the cloths, miss."

Shuffling noises tell me that Charlotte has handed the towels to Robert.

The unsure doctor immediately begins to stuff the towels into into my deep wound and press down firmly. Still, the blood flows. It soaks the towels and dribbles down the mattress to drip onto the floor. I can smell the blood and hear every drop ticking on the floor.

Charlotte tightens her grip on my hand. "It isn't working. He's dying."

I'm immortal, I want to assure her. But my voice won't work.

"Sorry, I'm not qualified for dealing with this level of trauma." Robert's voice has become shaky. "Anesthesiology isn't surgery."

Both Charlotte and Robert believe I won't survive. Cooper likely believes it too. He should know better. As a resident of the Outlands, he must realize what this place is and how it works.

The doctor's hands are trembling. Maybe he worries that his fate might be tied to mine, and if I die, he will too. Does Charlotte seem that terrifying to him? If so, Robert isn't a strong man.

"You've done your best," Charlotte tells Robert. "Please, go back to your wife. I'll handle this."

The speed of his footfalls tells me the man virtually sprinted out of the room.

"You can go too, Cooper," Charlotte says. "Shut the door behind you."

"Sure about that? I don't mind staying."

"Go on. I'll be fine."

The young man leaves with far less haste than Robert had exhibited. Cooper closes the door with only the barest click of the latch.

Charlotte removes the wadded-up towels and tosses them away. Blood still pours from my body, creating rivulets on the floor, I'm sure. My skin has grown clammy too, a new sensation for me. I've never lost this much blood before. How long will it be until I regain my strength? Lying in bed covered in blood is a new and unpleasant experience.

"Oh, God, Zane, how can I save you?" Charlotte sniffles. "Why do I want to save you is the better question. Can't explain it. All I know is that I don't want you to die. The medallion shouldn't have affected you this way."

She knows very little about me, and absolutely nothing about my physiology. That means the girl cannot conclude what the medallion should or should not do to me.

Charlotte sucks in a ragged breath. "My father had touched the medallion when he demanded Mum give it to him on the day they met, and the thing had burned his hand, nearly setting his trousers on fire. But the medallion had an entirely different effect on you. It burrowed inside your body, melting your flesh. How do I counteract that?"

Don't bother, I want to say.

"Only one thing comes to mind, but I can't believe it will work." She shifts position, making the mattress bounce. "But you will die if I don't do something, so I might as well give it a go."

Charlotte leans over me and sets a hand on the mattress beside my head. I can smell her natural scent that's both sweet and spicy, unlike anything I've detected from any other being. As her breaths whisper over my face, I feel my vigor beginning to return, if weakly. Charlotte seems determined to speed up the process.

Her lips brush across my mouth.

She'll need to do better than that to rouse me.

Charlotte presses her lips to mine more firmly, holding that position as if she's waiting for me to wake up and ravish her. At first, I can't respond. Then, as she molds her mouth to my lips, a soft groan emerges from me.

Sweet little Charlotte thrusts her tongue between my lips.

My skin grows warmer, but still, I can't move.

She settles her body on top of me, seeming not to care that she will have my blood covering her clothing and her exposed skin. Charlotte kisses me with even more fervor, moaning and grunting, desperate to taste me and awaken the demon within. She may regret trying to summon the beast in me. Sex with a demon isn't tender.

Suddenly, I realize more of my muscles have begun to function. I cup her ass with both hands, massaging those cheeks while a deep, guttural groan resonates through my chest. I can't stop myself from rocking my hips into her, teasing her cleft with my hard cock. I open my eyes to watch her expression while she ravishes my mouth and her stiff nipples scrape against my blood-soaked chest through the thin fabric of her nightie.

My powers have resurged. I'm in control again.

I push the girl off me and notice the blood that covers the front side of her body. No, I won't fuck her like that. But I need to sink my erection deep inside her as soon as possible. My cock demands it.

Leaping off the bed, I stomp over to the door and rip it open. "Clean this room at once, Lucy!"

"Right away, Zane."

I sweep Charlotte into my arms and teleport us to the only body of water within the confines of the Outlands. It lies on the far side of the Kevitash butte. The pool is rather small, though large enough to accommodate us both, and the water shimmers with the reflected silvery light of the moon. When I leap into the pool, Charlotte doesn't scream or seem even mildly surprised. I rip her chemise off and toss it onto the bank, then dispose of my own clothing in the same way.

Charlotte dunks her head under the water.

I pull her into my arms. "Let me cleanse your body."

"No thank you. I'd rather do it myself."

"Afraid my touch will arouse you too much, and you won't be able to stop yourself from begging me to take your body. That's right, isn't it?"

She twists her mouth into an irritated expression.

Yes, we both know I'm right about that. She couldn't resist me that night in her bedroom, which means she will succumb this time too.

I release my hold on her. "Float on your back, and I will cleanse you of the blood."

My blood. Why did she want to save me? That's a mystery I may never solve.

Charlotte obeys my command, now floating atop the gently lapping water of the pool. The moonlight casts its glow on her creamy skin and its faint freckles. The sight takes my breath away. My gaze travels over her body, from her rosy lips to the lovely round globes of her breasts. But the most enchanting aspect of Charlotte is her beautiful, mysterious irises that sometimes appear brown, sometimes green, and sometimes both simultaneously. Her skin is always milky yet dusted with faint freckles. In this lighting, she has the appearance of a goddess from Greek mythology, displaying her body for her lover.

"Why are you staring at me, Zane?"

"Because you are a vision of Greek beauty, like Aphrodite."

Her shoulders quiver, and she's clearly trying not to laugh at me. "A demon is poetic. I never would have expected that."

I ignore her statement and move to stand above her head. No, I don't need to float. I'm tall enough that my feet touch the bottom of the pool. As I slide my fingers into her blood-soaked hair, her lids flutter closed and a soft smile curls her lips. I gently massage her scalp as I wash away the blood, feeling myself relax too. When was the last time I felt that way? Never. Life in the underworld doesn't allow for downtime.

Once I've cleansed her hair, I scoop water into my cupped hands and drizzle it over her face. The red stains are washed away. I do the same for the rest of her body, and soon, Charlotte is clean.

Then I sink beneath the water to cleanse my entire body, whisking my hands through my hair to rid the strands of my own blood. My wound has healed. Because Charlotte wished it to do so? Or for some other reason? I don't care. My lust is overriding my common sense.

"Why have you been so polite about washing me off?" Charlotte asks. "It doesn't make sense. You're a puzzle I mean to solve."

"Don't bother. I'm a deformed demon who has no place in any world."

She glides her arms up and down on the surface of the pool. "You don't seem deformed to me."

"My horns have been forcibly removed. That is a disfigurement."

"What did your horns look like?"

I don't care to answer her question, not now, not ever. So, I move to stand at her feet. When she wriggles her perfect little toes, I bow my head to pull the largest digit into my mouth and wrap my tongue it around over and over. Charlotte sucks in a shallow breath. I've aroused her. *Perfect.* I tease her sole with two fingers while I continue suckling her toe, and I watch her expression as she grows more and more aroused. Even with the water surrounding us, I can still smell the delicious aroma of her desire.

"Zane, please, you should stop."

"Why? You enjoy what I'm doing."

"Yes, but—" She gasps when I push my head between her legs. "There must be wild animals out here."

"They are no match for a demon like me." I push further between her legs, my head now cradled by her creamy thighs. "I will pleasure you, right here, right now."

"What if I sink under the water?"

"That won't happen. Relax and enjoy the pleasure I can give you."

Her body goes slack, though it still floats atop the water. She keeps her gaze on me as I thrust my head further between her thighs, and the soft, curly hairs on her mound tickle my face. The scent of her overwhelms everything else, from the noises of insects to the lapping of the water. When I close my lips around her clitoris, she stops breathing, But when I latch on to that nub, her breaths quicken into soft, quick panting sounds.

I slide one finger inside her anus and thrust the thumb of that hand into her sheath.

Charlotte cries out.

My suckling grows more ravenous as I devour that little nub while grunting and growling. I fuck her with my thumb and that one finger, taking her from both sides while her cream dribbles down my hand. She thrashes and cries out, but she won't slip under the water. I will make certain of that. I can't silence my growls and grunts as they echo off the butte along with her desperate cries. My cock demands that I fuck her now, but I have other plans.

Her body clenches my thumb as her climax rockets through her entire body. I snarl and keep devouring her until she screams and then goes limp. Her chest heaves. She seems dazed too, as if the power of her orgasm shocked her.

Yes, a demon does do it better. Mortal men can't compete.

While Charlotte comes down from that high, I whisk us back to the ironclad room inside the saloon. The room has been cleansed of all signs of what happened here earlier. Drinking in Charlotte's pleasure has made me stronger, and my cock has grown thicker and longer than ever, ready to consume her body.

Lucy steps onto the threshold of the doorway. Her eyes flare wide. "You're all healed up."

"Yes." I drop Charlotte on the bed and stalk over to Lucy, shoving her backward with the palm of my hand on her chest. "Whatever you hear coming from this room, ignore it."

I slam the door and lock it. As I turn to face Charlotte, who lies sprawled on the recently cleaned bed, I can't move or speak. The beauty of her body, damp and creamy and flushed with speckles of pink, steals all of my focus.

She rises onto her elbows. "Are you going to chain me to the bed? To make sure I can't run away?"

"You won't do that." I open my mouth wide, drop the key onto my tongue, and swallow it. "See? You won't escape me."

"Swallowing an iron key doesn't seem like a good idea. It might rip your guts up."

I chuckle. "Demon, remember? Even your medallion can't kill me."

"What would you do if I said I don't want you to shag me tonight?"

"Change your mind, that's what I'll do." I shed my clothes and stalk over to the bed, then climb onto it. On hands and knees, I straddle the delicious little mortal. "You want this. We both know that. You need me to show you every filthy thing you've ever dreamed of but couldn't admit to aloud."

She glances around the room. "My father imprisoned my mother in this room. But he was a good man. You're a demon."

"Nathaniel Fortescue was a wolf. That means he was not a good man when he met your mother. He was, in fact, as much of a demon as I am, only in a different form." I slap a hand over her mouth to silence what I have no doubt would be a protestation that I am far worse than her father ever was. "No more talk of your family. It's time to turn sweet Charlotte into a wanton."

She peels my hand away from her mouth. "You keep saying that, but you don't do it. I think you aren't as evil as you want me to believe."

I bare my teeth and growl. "Then you are a foolish child."

Charlotte straps her arms over her chest. "Prove me wrong. Do something truly wicked." She lifts her chin. "Ravish me like the beast you claim to be."

She believes I won't do that. But the girl has no idea how much restraint I've needed to employ to stop myself from doing precisely what she suggested. Why am I holding back? If she wants a demon to ravish her, I'll give the girl what she wants. I've already locked us both inside this room. No more hesitation. It's time to rip away the restraints.

I rise to my knees, taking my cock in my hand, stroking it in a leisurely rhythm. Drops of liquid drip from the crown onto her skin as she bites her lip harder, turning it white. "Sit up, Charlotte, and take me into your mouth."

She pushes up into a sitting position and leans forward until her face hovers directly in front of my iron-hard erection. Charlotte licks her lips three times. Her pupils have blown, and her nipples have turned a tantalizing shade of rosy pink. She pulls in a breath and releases it gradually. Finally, she opens her mouth wide.

And the good girl takes me into her mouth as deep as she can.

I groan with relief. My cock still feels as if it might explode, but just having her mouth wrapped around my length relieves just enough of the pressure that I can let her do this as slowly as she likes. Sweet little Charlotte cups my sac with one hand while she reaches beneath my cock to gently rub the flesh behind my balls.

"Where did you learn this?" I growl. I can't speak normally anymore. Growling and snarling are the only options for me now. "How many men have fucked you?"

She draws her head back, releasing my dick. "I read about this in a book, and I wanted to use this technique on a boy I dated. He said he'd love for me to give him head, and I was determined to do it well." She stares at my erection with a hunger that makes me growl softly. "When I tried something like what I just did to you, he came instantly and couldn't get aroused again, not for hours. It was rather disappointing. He gave up and went home."

"That won't happen with me. I can get hard again in seconds."

"I believe it."

"You haven't answered my other question. How many men have enjoyed your body?"

"Four." She sets her hands on my hips, gazing up at me. "Why did you have sex with Lucy? Afterward, you treated her like rubbish."

"Lucy is a whore. She's used to being mistreated." I tap a finger on her lips. "And I only fucked her to increase my power. Sex and magics go hand in hand for a demon."

"Did you enjoy shagging her? You must have, otherwise you wouldn't have come for her."

Sweet Charlotte can't be jealous, but it's beginning to sound as if she is. The good girl envies a whore. "Don't worry. What I did with Lucy was quick and uninspiring, strictly a power grab, nothing more. She understood that."

"But she has a crush on you."

"No more talking unless it's filthy." I cup her chin in my hand. "Make me come, Charlotte. Suck me off like a wanton, like a whore."

She glowers at me. "I am not a prostitute."

"I said be *like* one, not become one. You know you want this, and I know it too. Give in to your wickedest instincts and suck me off."

CHAPTER TEN

Charlotte

As much as I hate that Zane is right, I can't deny he understands my needs better than I do. The men I've dated, and especially the ones I shagged, never wanted to try anything more than basic sex. I needed to explore my sexuality. But I wound up doing that on my own in my bedroom, secretly reading sex manuals and figuring out how to make myself come. I never would have expected that a demon would be the one to draw out my hidden passions.

I can't believe I'm doing this. With Zane. In this room.

Did Mum and Dad have sex on this exact same bed? I have no idea, and I would never ask them about their erotic adventures in the Outlands. I know they did get naughty together since I was conceived here in this wasteland.

My gaze has remained glued to the demon's cock. No point in fighting my impulses. Since I might die in this town, why not experience all the pleasure I can in the meantime?

I slide Zane's cock between my lips again. The flavor of his skin inundates my senses, both salty and spicy with a hint of decadent sweetness too. As I begin to pump his length with my mouth, I grasp the base of his cock to pump it from that end too. Zane groans with a depth of relief that makes my clit pulse. I slide my tongue round and round while I go on thrusting his length deep into my mouth until the tip touches the back of my throat. I love the way he hisses in a breath and then blows it out only to suck in another breath and repeat the process.

An idea strikes me, and I can't stop myself from enacting it. I pull my mouth away, but before Zane can chastise me, I push my breasts together and thrust forward. His cock glides between them, and the crown becomes visible. I've created a channel for him to thrust into, and he seems to appreciate my idea. While he thrusts between my breasts in an ever-quickening rhythm, I lower my mouth so I can lick his crown every time it emerges.

"Fuck, Charlotte, I need to come all over your tits."

"Do it, Zane, please. Then come inside my mouth too."

I've become so aroused that it's almost painful. The wickedness in me has taken hold fully, and I reach down to rub my clit while he thrusts between my breasts. Finally, he freezes, not even breathing. With one final thrust, he punches upward and sprays his seed all over my chest and throat. The searing heat of it makes me come. While I'm still orgasming, he flips me onto my back and plunges his length inside me so forcefully that I cry out. He's so big, so hard, that I feel as if he might rip me in two simply by shagging me.

The mattress bounces, and the bed itself thumps on the floor so hard that the whole thing moves. I grip the bed rails hard enough to make my knuckles ache. But I don't care. I go on begging him to never stop and to make me come over and over until I pass out. Is that really my voice shouting those words? I've gone barmy, for sure.

Zane hoists my hips and punches into me one last time. While his body goes rigid, I scream. The way he comes inside me, it's like nothing I ever imagined. My climax hits me so forcefully that it steals my breath away and my ears begin to ring, yet I still don't want the bliss to end.

He pulls out of me at last, breathing hard. "Charlotte? Are you alive?"

My eyes have shut of their own volition, but I can't understand why he asked if I'm alive. Shouldn't that be fairly obvious? A woman can't scream with ecstasy if she's dead.

Zane grasps my shoulders and shakes them. "Charlotte, open your eyes."

Lazily, I smile and peel my lids apart. "What are you on about now? I was enjoying the lovely afterglow."

The anguish on his face confuses me, but it vanishes quickly as he sits back on his heels and rubs a hand over his mouth. "You are alive, then."

"Of course I am." When I notice his hands are shaking, I push up onto my elbows and study him. "Did I miss something? Did a band of invisible brigands invade the bedroom while I was enjoying the bliss of the most incredible orgasm in the history of the world?"

He scowls at me. "Don't test my patience, woman."

"Then explain to me why you were so upset a second ago."

"I thought—" He knifes a hand through his hair. "Never mind."

"But I do mind. Tell me why—"

He jumps off the bed. "Do not harass me. When I tell you to forget about something, you will obey me."

"Because I've done that so often since we met." I sit up and scuttle backward until my back meets the bed rails. "Thank you for the amazing sex, but I am not your plaything."

"No, you are my property."

"Like hell you are. I am the daughter of an earl, which means you should refer to me by my title—Lady Charlotte."

He laughs bitterly. "In the underworld, the only title that matters is the name of the demon who sits on the throne."

I hadn't really expected him to accept my title. But he makes me so angry, and I wish I could find a way to tame him. Not bloody likely. So, I change my tactic. "I'm starved after all that exercise. You should at least want to keep me well-fed if you mean to shag me again, though I will never permit that."

"You want me again," he says in a low, throaty snarl. "I'll have you as many times as I like, in as many ways as I like, and you'll beg for more."

I roll my eyes. "That rubbish is getting old."

"The what? You're speaking nonsense."

"Oh, forget about it. I'm tired of explaining modern slang to you."

Zane stalks over to the window furthest from the bed, gazing down at who knows what. He can probably see in the dark, but I can't. Zane is the most confusing male of any species that I've met, and I can't unravel the riddle of him. Most of the boys I've dated were easy to read, so I had no trouble figuring out their motivations. Eat, shag, skedaddle. But the demon seems to be in no hurry to leave this room.

Well, that might have something to do with the fact that he swallowed the sodding room key.

As I gaze at Zane's backside, I can't resist admiring his body. That taut arse. Those massive biceps. His equally massive thighs. The reddish tinge of his skin gives him a mysterious aura, and I find myself entranced by the vision of his body as I skim my gaze over the rest of him. He seems always to be on edge, awaiting some terrible event. That must be what a demon's life is like. Never knowing when you might die. Never having a moment to relax. He probably sleeps with his eyes open.

Zane's own father had sawed off his horns. What sort of contemptible bounder treats his own son that way? I'm still having trouble adjusting to this new world. If I want to understand it, I'll need to ask an expert.

I walk up behind Zane and duck under his arm. Then I slide my arm around his waist. "What are you staring at? Are there demons roaming about?"

"Not that I'm aware of." He flicks his gaze down to me without lowering his head. "Why are you behaving in a friendly manner now?"

"Because I want to understand you and this world that I find myself trapped inside of. Will you answer a few questions for me?"

The tension in his body lessens a touch. "All right."

"Are we in a parallel world? Is that what the Outlands is?"

"Essentially, yes. But it's more than that. This parallel reality is infused with dark magics that can induce time travel and anything else that a powerful being might want."

"Anything? There must be rules for this world."

"Naturally. But only the most powerful beings can access the darkest magics, and a power beyond that of any demon or sorceress determines the rules."

"Really? Does that power belong to a god of the underworld?"

"No, it's a type of demonic energy that controls the entire Outlands and the underworld too."

I'm getting the impression that he doesn't actually know how it all works. Might as well move on to another issue. "Can you induce time travel? My mum was dragged into the past by magics, but she and my father still have no idea how that happened."

"You seem to be suggesting that I brought you here via time travel. I did not." Zane tugs me a little closer, though he seems unaware of the movement. "The Rom witch, Kezia, caused both of us to be pulled into the Outlands. Or as you seem to prefer to call it, Wrathrock."

"The Outlands is a cool name, but Wrathrock is much cooler." My mother loves to use the word cool, but Zane seems rather confused by it. I decide to explain to the demon who is ignorant of the modern world. "If I say something is 'cool,' it means I like it."

"Humans are strange animals. In the demon world 'cool' means that something is at a lower temperature."

"It means the same thing for mere mortals too, in addition to the other sense of the word." I sidle in front of him so that my body is now pressed against the windowsill and his large penis lies flaccid against my backside. When I peer down at what lies below us, I grow curious. "What is that small shed-like building down there?"

"The outhouse."

"Are you saying I didn't need to relieve myself in the chamber pot in this room? I could've gone down there to use the outhouse?"

"Yes."

I try to seem angry when I glance up at him, but I've never been terribly good at that. "Do you get off on watching a woman piss in a pot?"

"No. You never asked if there was another option for relieving yourself."

I grumble, muttering a curse under my breath.

Zane slides his hands around my waist, and further down until his big palms cover my groin. "You may use the outhouse whenever you like. But you might encounter men of the Outlands coming and going from that shed."

"I think I'll stick with the chamber pot for now." I wince. "Though I did accidentally dump the pot out on someone's head. It was Lucy, and she wasn't pleased."

"How did you know to dump out the chamber pot through the window? I never told you about that."

"Mum told me about that. She was in this room twenty-four years ago, you know."

He stiffens. "How could I have forgotten?"

"Because you weren't there."

Zane pulls away, backing up toward the bed. I turn around just as his knees meet the foot of the mattress. He stares at something beyond the window, or maybe something only he can see. It could be nothing at all. He's clearly disturbed by something in our conversation, but whether I said it or he did, I have no idea.

I approach him but remain a couple of arm's lengths away. "Zane, what's wrong? You look like you've seen a ghost."

He continues to stare out the window. "It might as well have been a ghost—of my own making."

"That doesn't make sense."

"It will soon enough."

His entire demeanor shifts in slow motion, as if he's realizing the import of whatever disturbed him. He straightens his posture, rolling his shoulders back. Then, he fists his hands. Clenches his jaw. Narrows his gaze. A red glow in his eyes begins as a smoldering flame, only to flare into a wildfire. When he speaks, his voice has become gravelly and as deep as the bowels of hell.

"You are a duplicitous little girl, Charlotte Fortescue of Wilderhampton. But I will never again step into one of your traps."

"I haven't set any traps." His dangerous demeanor makes my skin crawl. I realize I'm standing on top of a time bomb, and I need to defuse it. Blimey, I wish I'd studied to be an explosives expert instead of a schoolteacher. I keep my tone reassuring as I speak to Zane. "I don't want to trick you. Please tell me why you're angry, and maybe I can help you calm down."

"No more traps!" he shouts with so much volume that my ears hurt and the windows tremble. "You are the wolf's daughter. That is your only value to me. When I return you to your family, they will receive a broken girl who will be terrified of her own shadow. And it's time I stopped allowing you to thwart my plan."

A chill shimmies up spine, one so frigid it might be composed of shards of arctic ice. Zane has turned back into a vile demon, and I have no means of escaping this room or this world.

He surges forward, towering over me from less than a centimeter away. "When I come back, your violation will begin."

Zane stalks over to the door and wretches. The room key plops onto the wood floor. He snatches his clothes up, and the room key too, then stomps out the door. He locks it behind himself.

And I am trapped.

I stand here naked, afflicted with a chill that burrows deeper than the cold air inside this room. It has penetrated my very soul. Zane was trying to frighten me. I know that, but I can't understand why. How many times have I wondered about his actions and motivations? Only every minute since I was thrown into the Outlands. Being trapped in this world with an unstable demon, and imprisoned in an iron-clad room, I have zero options.

Like hell I do. I am the daughter of Kylie Drummond and Nathaniel Fortescue. And I have the Kevitash medallion. Yes, I will find a way to get home.

But first, I need some clothes.

CHAPTER ELEVEN

Zane

I STALK DOWN THE STAIRS WITH FOOTFALLS POUNDING SO LOUDLY that the entire stairwell shudders beneath my feet. My eyes must still be glowing with demonic fire too. Everyone in the saloon scatters as I stomp through the room, heading for the swinging doors. Lucy gapes at me with more horror than I've ever seen from any human. Robert, the doctor who attempted to save my life, sprints out the door ahead of me and rushes across the dusty street in the dark. Only the lights of the saloon would be burning now. It's nighttime, after all.

As I push through the swinging doors, Lucy approaches me from behind. "Zane, what's happened? Is that little girl…"

Dead. That's what she wanted to ask me. The answer is no, Lady Charlotte Fortescue has not died, not at my hands or anyone else's. But I don't feel like explaining myself to a saloon whore. "Leave me alone, Lucy. I know you're itching for me to fuck you again, but I've lost my taste for filthy hags like you."

"But, Zane—"

I whirl around and snarl at her like the rabid beast I am. "Shut your mouth before I rip your head off."

Lucy goes pale and scuffles backward into the saloon.

And I stalk out into the night, having no idea what I will do now. The moment I first saw Charlotte, my plans to ruin her and send the remnants back to her family had flown out the window. Why can't I follow through with my plan? Back in that room with Charlotte, I had suddenly realized what I've become. The former general of the collective armies of the demon hordes has become a lapdog for a tiny mortal female.

I halt at the edge of town to survey the area. Where am I going? No idea. Somehow, I must cow Charlotte. Yes, I've had great luck with that so far. She seems to be uncowable. And now I'm using an invented word like the ones Charlotte employs. A litany of vile curses tumble from my lips, and yet, I still feel emasculated.

One little female has done this to me.

I close my eyes, determined to tap into my magics and find a solution to the problem of Lady Charlotte. Instead, visions of her assail me. Naked Charlotte. Aroused. Writhing. Wet and ready for me to—

"Gah!" I bellow to the sky. Then I shove my hands into my hair, bow my head, and groan. "How can I get that woman under my thumb?"

Speaking to myself seems like a sign of insanity. Yes, Charlotte does drive me mad. My attempts to defile her resulted in me pleasuring her with my tongue and allowing her to take my cock into her mouth. Then I screwed the woman, and she loved it. Instead of dominating her, I succumbed to my hunger for Charlotte's body.

I need a new strategy.

As I shuffle further away from the town, I hear a wolf baying in the distance. Whether it's a mundane wolf or the supernatural kind, I can't tell. I stop and turn toward the direction of the mournful call. Every hair on my arms and at my nape lifts, inducing a slight shiver. Hearing that wolf's howling has stirred an idea. While I gaze up at the stars, the strategy unfolds in my mind until I've crafted the perfect plan. I need to take Charlotte to the one place that has the most significance for her parents.

The Kevitash butte.

I've learned enough about her to understand what that location means to her—and to Kylie and Nathaniel. This is the perfect way to mete out my vengeance.

The moon shines full and bright over the Outlands this evening. I won't need a torch to reach my destination.

I walk swiftly back to the saloon. When I enter the establishment, I ignore all the miscreants who are guzzling booze as if it were the elixir of life. I also ignore Lucy, who seems determined to annoy me with her whining. She wants me to ravish her. I have no taste for the wench, never did, and I only used her body to serve my magical needs.

Once I've raced up the stairs, taking them three at a time, I burst into the ironclad room and kick the door shut. I make sure to lock the door too.

Charlotte jumps, whirling toward me. "So, you decided to come back after all and grace me with your presence."

Her acerbic tone has the opposite effect from what she must have intended. Rather than annoying me, it makes me horny.

I halt an arm's length from the naked beauty. "You will need clothing. We're going to the Kevitash butte."

"Why? I don't need or want another bath with you."

Of course she wants that. She wants me, and we both know it. But I ignore her and holler, "Lucy! Bring clothes for the girl."

My voice booms deafeningly in the small room. Charlotte grimaces and covers her ears.

I stomp on the floor, making the whole room shiver. "Lucy! Right now!"

My chest is heaving. I can't silence the soft growls that emanate from me. The longer I'm forced to stare at Charlotte's nude body, the more my dick swells. Very soon I will be hard again and in need of a woman's body to slake my thirst.

Lucy gingerly pushes the door open and steps only far enough inside the room to hand me a wad of clothing. "They're the right size. Need anything else?"

"Only for you to leave us."

Lucy hustles out of the room, shutting the door.

I toss the clothing bundle to Charlotte. "Put these on. Do it quickly."

The infernal woman lifts her chin, giving me a haughty glare. "Suddenly in a hurry, are you? Sounds like you're desperate for another shag, but you won't be getting your end away with me."

"We are going to the butte. What makes you think that means I'll seduce you?"

"Because you'll take me to the pool again."

Ah, she thinks she knows everything about me. But Charlotte is wrong. "There will be no bathing in the pool this time. Now, get dressed—or I'll do it for you."

"Turn away, please, you vile brute."

I ignore her rude statement and acquiesce to her request only because I want to speed up the process. I can hear her hastily pulling on clothing, as evidenced by the rustling noises.

"You may look now, Zane. I'm dressed."

I turn around, and sheer fury overwhelms me. "Lucy, that conniving witch."

"Don't you like this?" Charlotte hoists her chin and sets her hands on her hips as she twirls for me. "I'd say it's appropriate for what you have in mind."

Lucy has given Charlotte a saloon girl's outfit. Her scarlet-red dress features only slender black straps to hold it up. The skirt portion extends down to the floor—except on one side, where the hem rises to barely below her groin. Her black lace-up boots have high heels. The way her hair is draped behind one shoulder but cascades over the other makes me growl softly. The whole blasted outfit does that to me.

And Lucy knew that would happen. I should punish her immediately, but chastising the wench for her impudence will need to wait until later.

I seize Charlotte's arm. "Let's go. And I do not want to hear a word from you unless I give you permission to speak."

She raises her brows.

I drag her out of the room, down the stairs, and through the saloon. No one dares to complain about my behavior. I control the Outlands, after all. Rahn'omith might believe he owns this domain, but it belonged to my father and therefore belongs to me as well. I keep walking, towing the girl along with me, until we reach the periphery of the town.

"Are we leaving Wrathrock?" she asks.

"Yes."

She smirks. "You tacitly admitted that this place is called Wrathrock."

"We need to call this town something, I suppose. Might as well stick with the tourists' name for it." When she smirks again, I squeeze her arm tightly enough to make her gasp. "This is not a humorous situation. I am enraged. Behave accordingly. And you will close your mouth until I give you permission to speak. One more infraction and I will discipline you."

Charlotte makes a zipper motion across her lips.

I hoist her into my arms and leap into the air.

She gasps again while I send us higher and higher into the atmosphere until we reach the appropriate height. Then I send us plummeting downward. We hurtle ever closer to the ground, and Charlotte hugs me tightly while biting down hard on her lips. I've transported us in this manner before. She shouldn't find it so jarring this time, but she clearly does.

I slow our descent as we approach the ground, setting us down as gently as possible. "We are here. The remainder of our journey will take us inside the butte."

"You don't want to go in there. It's Kevitash territory, and they don't appreciate uninvited visitors."

"The Kevitash are dead. Their magics linger here, but they're available to anyone who possesses the power to harness them."

I lash my hand to her wrist as we navigate around the vertical slab of rock that hides the entrance to the hidden passage. The slab is attached to the butte, and we easily wend our way past it. Once inside the corridor, we remain cloaked in a deep darkness with no sign of light in either direction. I know the route to the Kevitash chamber by heart, having walked it several times during my father's reign as king. This place might have changed in the intervening years.

Soon, we begin to see glimmers of light up ahead. We're almost there.

Charlotte trips and curses under her breath. My hand on her arm stays her fall. I have better sight in the dark than she does and the benefit of muscle memory. Despite suffering a strong impulse to ask if she has injured herself, I stop short of doing that. Showing even a sliver of courtesy to her has proved dangerous. Charlotte Fortescue is wilier than I expected.

I bump into the wall, simply because the passage narrows here. It's the entrance to the Kevitash chamber. I halt. "Remain in this exact spot. Do not move even one inch. I'm about to enter the chamber and light the lantern that should still be here, hanging on the wall."

"Yes, I know about that. My parents told me."

Naturally, she's aware of this hidden chamber. I expected as much. "Do not move from this location."

"All right. I'll do as you command, even though I don't appreciate your snarly tone."

She loves my "snarly" tone. I can smell how aroused she gets when I behave like a demonic jackass. But I don't care to argue with her about that right now. Without too much fumbling around, I find the lantern and light the wick.

A warm, golden glow illuminates the chamber.

Charlotte shuffles over the threshold and studies the chamber with a look of awe on her face. "This is amazing. It's a good thing there were still matches for you to use. My father left them here."

"I did not use a match."

"Then how did you light the lantern?"

"With my fingers." Since she clearly doesn't believe that, I demonstrate for her by flicking my forefinger across the pad of my thumb. A small flame erupts. "That is how I lit the lantern."

Her eyes widen. "Oh. That's...an interesting way to light a flame."

"And it arouses you."

She rolls her eyes. "You're obsessed with sex. But no, I am not turned on by your ability to use your fingers like a matchbox." She cants her head to the side. "Can you see in the dark?"

"I'm not a wolf. Demons can't see in pitch darkness, though we do have modest night vision. Utter darkness is different."

"How fascinating." Her tone suggests she's being sarcastic. "Why have you dragged me to this cavern?"

"To enact my evil plan, of course."

She stares at me for a moment as if she can't decide whether I'm being sarcastic. Then a sigh rushes out of her, and she shuffles a few more paces into the small chamber. "Your sense of humor needs work. I suppose demons aren't required to have wit or charm. All you do is murder and shag."

"We also raise children and maintain a hierarchy not unlike human royalty—or the armed forces in your world."

Charlotte moves into the center of the chamber and faces the paintings on the wall. "Blimey. I can't believe I'm actually here in the chamber my parents visited twenty-four years ago. Mum and Dad wouldn't tell me all the details, though I figured out they had sex in this cavern. All they would say was that the Kevitash butte and the chamber inside it played a vital role in Mum saving Dad from being killed by Zor'imuth."

She glances at me over her shoulder, as if she expects me to rail against her mother for destroying my father. I might want to avenge that act, but I despised my father. Kylie Drummond did me a favor. But I cannot let Rahn'omith control the demon hordes. That is why I must avenge my father's death.

Only then can I seize control of the underworld.

CHAPTER TWELVE

Charlotte

"HOW MUCH DO YOU KNOW ABOUT THE KEVITASH?" I ASK AS I MOVE closer to the cave wall, entranced by the images painted onto the surface. Whether Zane will answer my question, I won't know until he chooses to speak again. For the past few minutes, he's done nothing but stare at the wall. Is he entranced by the figures painted on the wall too? Who knows.

Zane comes up alongside me. "I have little knowledge of the Kevitash. My father didn't like to talk about them."

"Would you care to learn more?"

He jerks as if I've slapped him. "You would share that information with me?"

"Only enough so that you'll understand their power. You won't trick me into revealing all their secrets."

"How could you know their secrets? You have never visited this place before."

I fold my arms over my chest and shake my head at him. "I just explained how I know. Are you going deaf?"

"Silence, child," he snarls. "You are nothing more than a tool for achieving my goals."

"You mean to ravish me so thoroughly that I'll be a mindless wanton, incapable of denying you anything. Isn't that right?"

A muscle ticks in his jaw. "Wrong."

Harassing a demon might seem like a foolish thing to do, but I have nothing to lose anymore. I will probably need his help to bring the Kevitash paintings to life. I'm not sure I have the innate magics that Mum tapped into when she animated the images. Honestly, I'm flying blind here.

What would Mum do? She's a very clever woman, and a strong one too. She reined Dad in and helped him become the man he was always meant to be. I don't want to give Zane a morale boost so he can become a better demon. That would be a bloody stupid thing to do. I had started to like him, a little bit, but he ruined that. And right now, I'm more concerned with what his evil plan involves and how it affects me.

At least I have the medallion tucked inside my bodice.

Yes, that's terribly helpful when I have no ruddy idea how to use it. Maybe I should have let the medallion melt Zane into a puddle of demonic slime.

"The first thing you should know about the Kevitash," I tell him, "is that your father murdered every last member of their tribe."

That muscle in his jaw ticks again. "I'm aware of my father's genocidal tendencies."

"And do you approve of his methods?"

"You're supposed to tell me about the Kevitash, not interrogate me."

I glance at him and shake my head, then sigh as I face the paintings again. "Do you know the whole story about your father's atrocities?"

Zane's entire body has become as stiff as a steel bar. He glowers at the wall while fisting and loosening his hands over and over again. "Zor'imuth destroyed the Kevitash. My father often bragged about his accomplishment. He killed many of the Rom too, particularly Erosabel's kin."

"Your father abducted Erosabel." I study the paintings, allowing my gaze to wander wherever it wants to go. "Her family sent her across the ocean on a raft in the hopes she would land in a better place and be safe. It was the only chance she had of escaping the demon prince."

"My father was king, not prince."

"But he started out as a prince. How do you not know that? Zor'imuth was your father."

Zane turns his head away slightly, just enough to convey the fact that he doesn't like talking about Zor'imuth. "Once I reached adulthood, I was named general of the army of the demon hordes. That meant I was relegated to the deepest levels of the underworld and had virtually no contact with my father."

Maybe I had prodded him into discussing his father, but it was the only way to get him to talk. I don't believe he really wants to turn me into a broken lump of flesh who will be his eternal slave. I do worry that my attempts to make him open up might lead me into treacherous territory. He isn't entirely stable, that much I know.

"I'm sorry you had to live that way, Zane."

He flashes me a dark look. "Do not pity me."

"No chance of that." I gaze intently at the paintings, willing them to come to life as they had for my mother so long ago. Nothing happens. Maybe I'm trying too hard and need to let the images awaken on their own. "Pay attention to this. You need to see what your father did to Erosabel and her clan."

"Crude paintings will show me nothing."

"Look at the wall, Zane. Watch and wait."

His eyes narrow to slits, but he aims his gaze at the paintings.

Mum loves to tell me the story of what happened in this chamber twenty-four years ago, and now the words echo in my mind. My father had told her how to access the moving images on the stone wall. *These drawings relate the story of Erosabel and Rohnesh, he had said. Look at the images. Don't think, simply let them penetrate your mind, and the story will unfold before your eyes.*

The images begin to shimmer, but they don't become animated.

Mum had told me that Dad set his hands on her shoulders while they both watched the cave wall. I wonder if it takes contact from two people to enliven the images. I glance at Zane peripherally. He might get angry if I touch him, but I need to try.

So, I reach out to clasp his hand.

He flinches. But then, the snarling demon gently threads his fingers with mine, and we both fixate our gaze on the artwork.

The images begin to move, dancing across the wall as if they're living things.

"What is happening?" Zane asks, his voice hushed.

"The story is about to begin. See those two people, a man and a woman who are holding hands? That's Erosabel and Rohnesh. You see, when Erosabel landed in North America, she wandered for many years until she found herself in what is today called Utah. The Kevitash tribe took her in, and eventually, she married a Kevitash warrior called Rohnesh and bore children."

The pictures on the wall move in time with my narration. It's an eerie thing to watch, yet also beautiful and intriguing.

Zane clasps my hand more firmly.

"Many years later, your father found Erosabel again. He threatened to take her back to his demon kingdom." I suddenly realize I've inched closer to Zane without meaning to do that. Still, I feel oddly safer watching these images with him beside me. "Rohnesh tried to stop Zor'imuth from taking Erosabel, but he was nearly killed in the battle. To save the man she loved, she made a deal with your father. If he would heal Rohnesh and stay away from her children, she would go with him. But Erosabel was no fool. She tricked Zor'imuth."

"No one tricks a demon king and lives to tell the tale."

"You don't know the women in my family." I let my focus wander wherever the images take me as I relate the rest of the story. "Erosabel marshaled all the magics of the Rom and the Kevitash to strip Zor'imuth of his powers and turn him into a human man, though he became the first werewolf."

"What became of Erosabel?"

"In her bid to stop Zor'imuth, all the life was drained from her body. But her soul lived on, and she—"

"What did she do? You stopped speaking mid-sentence."

Am I hallucinating, or did the demon seem anxious to hear the rest of the story? I can't tell him the next bit. He might misuse the information. But on the wall, the images continue to unfold, and the remainder of the tale plays out before our eyes anyway. I bite my bottom lip, trying not to give away the importance of the events depicted in the living images. But I'm a ruddy awful liar, and Zane is too clever by half.

"Erosabel created the medallion, didn't she?"

I wince hard enough that I can barely see Zane through my slitted eyes. "Yes, she did. The medallion holds within it the essence of the curse. Or, it used to. My parents believe the medallion has no power anymore."

"But you know it does. That's how it was able to melt my flesh."

"Yes, you're right about that. Mum and Dad were wrong."

"Or perhaps the medallion was reactivated when you were thrown into the Outlands."

I stand by my assertion that Zane is too clever by half. It makes me uneasy but also turns me on.

No more sex with the demon.

The images on the wall return to their original positions and cease moving. That part of the story is over, but I might as well share the rest with Zane. "After Erosabel delivered her last gift to her people, the Kevitash and the Rom understood that the curse's power would exact a hefty toll on the Kevitash. The tribe could no longer produce any children. Their lineage died out, though Rohnesh and his brothers lived on, as did their descendants, through their connection with the Rom. But I've never understood what that means."

"If all the Kevitash were cursed to have no children, then Rohnesh could have no descendants."

"But the story claims they did. It's a confusing contradiction." I scrutinize the part of the painting that depicts Erosabel enacting her curse and try to understand the cryptic final moment. "My father also told me that a Ute elder told him Rohnesh and Erosabel were banished after she cast her spell. They traveled back to their homeland in the Old World, and their lineage continued. All female descendants are known as the Daughters of Erosabel."

"Perhaps the gypsies crafted a deliberately indecipherable story."

"Why would they do that?"

"To hide a deeper truth and protect their descendants."

For a moment, all I can do is gawp at the demon. His keen insights make me feel useless. Might that be the reason why Zane and I were thrown into the Outlands together, by a Rom witch? She might be trying to teach us both a lesson that will lead us to uncover the deeper truths about the Kevitash and their kin, the Daughters of Erosabel.

"You are a descendant of Erosabel. Aren't you, Charlotte?"

"I am. So was my mother. I have no idea how far back our connection to the Rom and the Kevitash goes."

"We should explore that association." Zane turns toward me, still holding my hand, and hooks a finger under my chin. He rotates my head so we're eye to eye. "As much as I would like to help you discover more about your lineage, I need to ask you another question."

The fact that he wants to help leaves me stunned briefly. Then I swallow against the lump in my throat. "Go on. Ask me."

"Do you know how my father became king? If he was cursed to live as a mere mortal, albeit one who was also a werewolf, he could not rule the underworld. Yet he did rule. For all of my existence, Zor'imuth was the king of the demon hordes."

"You must have been born after his curse was lifted."

"I was born long before that. But I didn't see my father for many centuries, including the day he died. He shunned me."

Staring straight into his glowing red eyes is disconcerting, but I refuse to look away. That would be a sign of weakness. "Cordelia, an evil cow who was also a wolf, found a way to rid Zor'imuth of his curse. He became a demon again. Then, he murdered his father and claimed the throne."

Zane's red gaze bores into mine. "My father used to speak of a wolf called Cordelia. He laughed at what a fool she was."

I huff. "Cordelia Atherton deserved what she got. That woman tried to kill my mother, but Dad grabbed a rifle and shot her. She was in wolf form at the time."

"A bullet can destroy a werewolf? I've never heard that before."

"It's true. Cordelia was taken down by an old-fashioned rifle. No magic required."

Zane's attention swerves to the paintings. He releases my chin, rotating his body toward the wall, and pulls in a deep breath. As he scrutinizes the images, he exhales that breath little by little. The red glow in his eyes lessens. He raises both arms, palms out.

A chill slithers up my spine. "What are you doing, Zane?"

"Thank you for sharing that story with me. The information will enhance the spell."

"What spell?" Another shiver rushes over my skin, rattling me down to my bones. I force myself to maintain a calm yet resolute tone. "Zane, why are you trying to cast a spell? For what purpose?"

He rests his palms on the wall. "This is my vengeance."

"I don't understand. The paintings were created by magics, by the Kevitash and the Rom."

Zane's lips peel away from his gritted teeth as he speaks in a low, snarling tone. "I will invoke demonic magics, nothing like the kind Erosabel and her kin summoned. It is time to wreak my vengeance on those who destroyed my father."

"But you hated him. He treated you cruelly. Why on earth would you want to continue his quest for vengeance against the Rom? The Kevitash are long gone, so there is no one else to punish."

He swerves his head toward me, and his nostrils flare. "If you speak again, I will gag you."

I've witnessed this side of him before, and I know he behaves this way when he's afraid. Of me? I'm not sure. Maybe he's afraid to admit he cares for me, and maybe that's because he worries about what his fellow demons might do to him if they find out he has tender feelings for a mere mortal. A girl, no less.

Do they have female demons? I imagine they must. Otherwise, it would be quite difficult for them to procreate. I've had sex with Zane. What if I'm up the duff? Can a human survive giving birth to a half demon? No, I can't worry about that right now. I'm more concerned with what this demon is plotting.

I need to coax him into giving up this mad scheme. That means I need to placate him. "Zane, please help me understand what you're about. What you're trying to accomplish."

"Revenge. How many times must I tell you that? You're a stupid girl, aren't you?"

"Snarling at me is not the way to gain my cooperation."

"I don't need you to cooperate." He still has his palms on the wall, but now he begins to grunt softly. "Your desecration will be my retribution."

CHAPTER THIRTEEN

Zane

I DON'T KNOW WHAT I'M DOING ANYMORE, MUCH LESS WHY I'M determined to finish what I started. I'd resolved to find Charlotte and turn her into a wanton, a slave to my lust for her. Yet I've only fucked her once, and it wasn't anything close to vile or shameful. I've been easy on her. She loved the feel of my cock inside her, and she doesn't seem at all fazed by the savage way I took her body.

"Zane, please talk to me."

No, I can't speak to or look at Charlotte. It's time to become the demon my father never believed I would be and mete out the proper punishment. Kylie Drummond and Nathaniel Fortescue must suffer. It's what my father would want.

You hated him. He treated you cruelly. Why on earth would you want to continue his quest for vengeance against the Rom?

Charlotte's words echo in my mind, but I cannot listen to her. Too much is at stake. Such as what? Claiming the underworld, a place I've hated for my entire life? Thinking will do me no good. It's time for action.

I bend my arms until my lips brush the rock wall. As I begin to chant softly in the demon tongue, I can see Charlotte out of the corner of my eye. Her brows have knit together over her nose, and she bites down on her bottom lip. The more I chant, the more she begins to nibble on her lip. She hugs herself too, though she doesn't even attempt to run away. I'm vulnerable right now, a fact I will not apprise her of. Invoking demonic magics requires a depth of concentration no mortal could possibly comprehend.

The dark energies bleed out of the rock and into me. They slither up my arms and neck, then spread up into my head and down through the rest of my body, sizzling and crackling inside me. My chanting becomes deeper and rougher, more mumbling than actual words. That doesn't matter. The magics don't care how I speak the words as long as I invoke the right spell.

"Zane?" Charlotte sounds anxious. I hear her shuffling backward. "Zane, what are you doing? I don't like this."

I ignore her statement and push harder into the magics, now growling the phrases while gnashing my teeth.

"Please, don't do this, whatever it is," Charlotte pleads. "These are black magics, aren't they? It's too bloody dangerous to try—"

Those dark energies have now enveloped me. To her, I must look like a man-shaped shadow within the roiling magics. I walk backward until I stand at the exact center of the chamber. Then, I raise my arms and spread my hands, palms up.

Footsteps patter across the floor behind me. Sweet little Charlotte is trying to escape. She shouts and hits the floor—on her ass, I assume.

I gradually turn around. Charlotte does indeed lie sprawled on her backside with her hair feathered over her face. The magics I've ingested have intensified my lust for her, but I won't claim her body just yet. I need to stain her soul first.

Charlotte scrambles to her feet. She seems wary of me, probably because, for once, I look like a true demon. Surrounded by slithering black energy. Suffused with dark spells. Nothing can stop me now. She scurries away from me until her backside meets the stone barrier of the cavern. Her gaze flicks to the painting on the wall behind me, which no longer portrays the travails of Erosabel and her lover, Rohnesh. Now, it displays images of demons and wraiths and every sort of evil being. They dance and writhe, screw and kill, commit every variety of despicable acts.

"What have you done to yourself, Zane?" Charlotte doesn't cower against the wall, to my surprise. Instead, she stands straight and meets my gaze head on. "You didn't need to do this. Dark magics will ruin you."

"I was ruined the day I was born. Demon, remember? We aren't known for our noble tendencies."

"But I've seen other sides of you. I know you have so much pain inside you because of what your father did to you." She takes half a step toward me. "Reject the dark magics and be with me."

No, she can't want me, not legitimately. She's only saying these things in the hopes that I'll give up my plan. I slant toward her until our gazes collide. "Humans have a tradition called Halloween."

"Yes, we do."

"The mortal holiday is a farce." I move closer, towering over her. "The real version is nothing like that. No silly masks. No toys shaped like devils. You are about to enter the domain of real demons, in the depths of actual hell."

She swallows hard. "If that's what it takes for me to break through your impenetrable shell and save you from yourself, then I will go into hell with you."

I chuckle. "Save me? You are a fool, sweet Charlotte."

"Maybe I am. Let's get on with it. Take me into the underworld."

She seems unusually anxious to go into the depths of the demon world. Considering how intelligent Charlotte is, I'm beginning to suspect she has an ulterior motive. I seize her arm, dragging her out of the chamber and down the long passageway. The walls have become infused with shimmering red veins of demonic energy. I can feel those veins pulsating, their power permeating the passageway. It rouses my carnal hunger. But I need to tamp it down for now, until I have Charlotte exactly where I want her.

Once we exit the passage and duck around the pillar that hides the cave entrance, I halt.

"Why have you stopped?" Charlotte demands. "Take me to your demonic lair so you can ravish me into submission. That's your master plan, isn't it? A ruddy stupid one if you ask me."

I glower at her, my teeth clenched. "I didn't ask for your opinion, little girl."

She huffs and gives me a haughty glare.

That also arouses me, and she has no idea how close I am to throwing her on the ground and slamming my cock inside her. But I won't do that here. Although I've started the process of corrupting her, I need to finish it in the underworld where the most intense magics live.

I seize her wrist and drag the woman out into the fresh air. Even a demon appreciates a good draft of the desert scent. It's unique and almost sweet. Charlotte trips repeatedly as I haul her around the far side of the butte. She curses under her breath and glowers at me several times too. Her insolence heats my blood and awakens my lust. That makes me grunt and growl softly, over and over while I struggle to maintain my wits just long enough to get this task done.

The butte has begun to hum with the energies I awakened in the rocks. Charlotte won't have noticed that. It's what mortals call infrasound, meaning a very low noise that most humans can't consciously detect. The frequencies within the butte seep inside me too, awakening my powers in ways I can't summon on my own.

I stop us in front of a particular section of rock.

Charlotte eyes the rock with suspicion. "Are you going to stare at this wall for a while too? I don't see any rock paintings that might dance for you."

"Be quiet, or I will seal your mouth with duct tape."

"Demons know about duct tape? Well, I'll be."

I squint at her. "You will be what?"

She rolls her eyes, as she often does. "It's a saying. My mum uses that phrase to mean that something has surprised her."

Humans are bizarre creatures. But their strange manner of speaking is irrelevant at the moment.

Charlotte lifts her brows. "You haven't duct taped my mouth yet. I did speak without your permission, after all."

A low growl rumbles in my chest. "Speak no more. We are about to ascend the butte, so I doubt you'll have the energy for harassing me."

She opens her mouth to complain but clearly thinks better of it, clamping her lips together.

And I drag her up the butte. It has a staircase of sorts, though the natural landscape has obscured it just enough to prevent nosy mortals from trying to hike up the rather steep slope. The staircase begins fifteen feet above the desert floor, after all, where the eastern face is a sheer vertical drop. I sweep Charlotte into my arms and leap into the air, flying up high enough to whump down at the base of the rock staircase.

Then I set Charlotte on her feet. "Do not attempt to flee, little girl. I can run and jump faster than any human."

She opens her mouth.

I slap a hand over it. "Do not speak."

Her lips pucker, which I know because I can feel it beneath my palm.

I give her a shove toward the staircase. "Ladies first."

Her seething glare has no effect on me, and she grudgingly begins the long climb up the steps. I try to keep my focus on the staircase ahead of us, but the way her buttocks flex with every step distracts me. The dress Lucy had chosen for Charlotte hugs her ass. I also get glimpses of her upper thighs. When Charlotte slips, but catches herself before she can fall, I receive a tantalizing glimpse of her nude buttocks.

But when she hoists her skirts, I can't squelch the ravenous growl that bursts out of me. She lifted her skirts to avoid tripping over them again. I know this, but my body doesn't care about the reason. It only knows that I need to bury myself inside her body again as soon as possible.

She glances back at me, seeming wary.

"I won't devour you, sweet Charlotte. Not yet."

We climb the steep stairs, mounting sixty-six rock steps along the way. By the time we reach the thirtieth step, Charlotte's pace slows down. She keeps going, though, clearly determined not to show any weakness. But a human female can't climb this many steep steps, not even if she trained for years before attempting the feat. At the thirty-eighth step, Charlotte gives up on holding her skirts up and simply struggles to remain on her feet. Her breaths come hard and fast. I can see her pulse throbbing in her throat.

On the fortieth step, she collapses.

I tower over her, considering my options. Though I had wanted to punish her with this trek up the butte, exhausting her was not part of my plan.

"Can't do it anymore, Zane." She struggles to breathe, and her face has turned red. "Haven't slept in I don't know how long. Nothing to eat or drink either. Maybe a demon doesn't need those things, but I do."

She sounds...defeated and exhausted.

I clench my fists over and over, studying the girl while I struggle to decide what to do. Kindness isn't appropriate, not for a demon. Yet I have previously shown her moderate kindness. It's weakness, though. Yet I need to get her up the butte to perform the required rituals.

A sigh blusters out of me—and I sweep her up in my arms.

No longer encumbered by forcing her to climb the staircase on her own, I race up the steps, leaping over several at a time. We reach the last step and find ourselves standing on a small platform carved out of the butte itself. I keep Charlotte nestled in my embrace as I chant the requisite words.

The air shimmers around us.

Charlotte clings to me with her face buried against my chest. Her fingers curl. Her breathing and her pulse both speed up. She has sensed the magics I'm invoking, though she has no idea of what it involves.

The world shifts around us.

"You may open your eyes now, Charlotte."

She peels one eyelid open, still clinging to me. Then her eyes go wide. She lifts her head to gawk at our surroundings. "I can't believe—This is hell?"

"We're in the underworld. It's not the same thing as hell with a capital H." I set her down on her feet. "This is my lair."

She whips her head around to gawk at me this time. "You live here?"

"Are you surprised that a demon has a home? You probably assumed I lived in a seething cesspit."

"No. Honestly, I never thought about where you lived."

I strip off my shirt and toss it away. "Undress, now."

"What if I refuse to obey you? You can go on and duct tape me now because I will not stop speaking."

As I remove the rest of my clothes, I watch her expression. It mutates from irritation to interest, and finally, clear sexual desire. "I'll have you naked one way or another, sweet Charlotte. Strip or be stripped. It's your choice."

CHAPTER FOURTEEN

Charlotte

THE ROUGH AND GROWLY TONE OF ZANE'S VOICE BOTH IRRITATES and excites me. My body loves it. My intellect says I should slap him in the face and knee him in the groin for behaving like a caveman. Dragging me up a mountain? Straight into the demon's lair? Zane takes the term alpha male to new heights. I wonder if my father behaved this way when he and Mum... No, I do not want to think about my parents shagging. It's too weird.

Zane stands before me completely nude—and fully aroused.

I glance around the lair, which is nothing more than a small cavern. Zane has a bed that looks surprisingly comfortable and not at all what I expected from a demon. Until the day Zane abducted me, I'd assumed that if real demons existed, they would resemble the creatures in horror films. Ugly. Revolting. Crude. Somewhere between a zombie and a vampire with fangs that drip blood. Yes, I've discovered recently that I have a morbid imagination.

And I blame it all on Zane.

I don't see any doors or vents for bringing clean air into the space. Do demons not need to breathe? That's hardly the most immediate concern for me, though. My mind keeps conjuring visions of all the vile things that Zane claims he's going to do to me. I wrap my arms around myself, but the chill I feel resides within me.

"Strip, Charlotte. Do it now. This is your last warning."

A loud boom detonates from somewhere further away. The walls tremble. Bits of rock shower down on the floor.

I hold perfectly still, afraid to move. "What the bloody hell was that?"

"The underworld is a violent place. Just wait until you hear the screams."

Oh, yes, this horrible domain sounds better and better every moment.

Zane's entire body seems taut and energized, like a high-tension power line. "I said strip, Charlotte. *Now.*"

Why fight? I have no way out of this literal hellhole unless he chooses to release me. So, I get rid of my clothes. "Should I lie down on the bed?"

"No." He rakes his gaze over me from head to toe, and his chest begins to heave with every growling breath he takes. "You won't get a soft bed until I'm done with you."

I'd thought I would feel odd about standing here naked with him studying my body, like a lion working out the best moment to pounce on a gazelle. But I don't feel odd about it at all. Instead, I feel a sense of power. That's barmy, for sure. Yet it seems right. I do have power over Zane, don't I? After all, he wants to shag me. Desperately. And he's gone to a bloody lot of trouble to gather a huge amount of magics and transport me to this lair, all so he could have me alone in this cavern.

"Up against the wall," he snarls. "Do it now."

"The whole room is one big curving wall. Which part of it should I lean against?"

He thrusts an arm out to point toward the wall opposite the bed. "That one. Quickly."

The demon really can't wait to shag me. That might be flattering under different circumstances. But I do as the arse commanded and approach the spot he'd indicated. "What now?"

He wipes a bead of sweat from his brow. "Turn around. Spread your legs and keep your hands on the wall."

This is beginning to feel like a police drama series, where the perpetrators have to stand like this to be frisked. When

I glance over my shoulder at Zane, he still stands there in that same spot, sweating and clearly confused. I'm not at all sure he knows what he means to do to me. The "plan" he kept touting seems to have evaporated.

Zane shuffles up behind me. His feet scrape across the floor.

I twist my head around to see him. The demon has halted an arm's length away. "I'm ready whenever you are, Zane. Ravish me."

"You should be frightened, little girl. The things I will do to you..."

"We had sex once before. Or are you so addle-brained that you can't remember? I know what shagging you will be like, so forget all your blustering nonsense and just do it."

To prove I mean what I said, I spread my legs even further and thrust my hips out. That gives him clear access to my body. I can hear his ragged breaths, though I can't see him since I'm facing the wall. When I do look over my shoulder, his expression of unadulterated lust makes my clit pulsate.

Zane growls as he lays his palms on my bottom.

I wriggle my arse.

He growls again, massaging my bottom roughly. When he pushes a finger between my cheeks, he can feel how wet I am. I don't need to see his expression to know that. My cream is dribbling down my inner thighs. He glides that finger between my folds, taking his time, which seems odd considering how intensely aroused he is. Zane keeps petting me that way for a moment, then he gently slides one finger inside me.

I gasp.

"You crave me, Charlotte. And I'll take you any way I want."

I gasp again as he pushes a second finger inside me. "Please, yes, I want you, full stop."

He retracts his fingers, then scrapes his nails up my arse. "Time to initiate you."

Whatever that means, I have no brainpower to understand it.

Zane pins me to the wall with his body. His hands cuff my wrists. He grunts like an animal as he sniffs my throat while rubbing his cock up and down my backside, from my arse cheeks to midway up my spine. "You are mine, sweet little Charlotte. Mine forever."

I manage to turn my head just enough that I can glimpse his face. His flesh has turned redder, and his eyes burn with a white-hot fire even while sparks of red flame ignite within them. Despite the changes in his eyes and skin, he still seems relatively human. Maybe that fact explains why I'm not only letting him ravish me, but I'm also desperate for him to do that to me.

Zane bites my neck gently. "Say it, Charlotte."

What does he want me to say? I can't think, and the truth I've tried to deny spills from my lips. "I'm yours forever, Zane."

He shoves one hand between my body and the wall, cupping my groin. His huge palm covers all of that area and more. When he pushes his hand between my folds, and even lower, the heat of his flesh alone makes me almost come. He keeps me pinned to the wall while he slides his cock between my legs ever so slowly until the tip emerges from my folds. My fingers curl into the wall, and my pulse accelerates more with every leisurely thrust. But when he pulls back and lunges his length into my sheath, I cry out because it feels so bloody good. None of the boys I dated ever wanted to take me from behind like this. They weren't adventurous at all.

Zane pulls out and flips me around to face him. He crushes me to the wall again, cuffing my wrists with his hand as he'd done earlier. But now, he spreads my thighs and plunges his cock inside me, holding that position for so long that I begin to feel lightheaded from the anticipation. I can't breathe again until he does something.

He undulates his hips in a circular motion. The unusual move lets his cock touch parts of me that have never been touched before. He's buried so deeply inside me that it takes my breath away. Sweat beads on his forehead, dribbling down his temples. Why is he fighting so hard to hold back? I need him to let go, so I writhe against him. The movement rubs my nipples over his chest.

"Please fuck me the demon way, Zane. Stop holding back. Show me everything you can do."

He freezes, his gaze nailed to mine.

I brush my lips over his. "Do it, Zane."

A groan deeper than anything I've ever heard resonates in his chest. Then, he finally does it. He staggers backward until we're away from the wall, and he splays both his palms on my back, lowering me until I'm hanging in the air. My hair fans out below my head. I can't touch him because I can't reach him. But he still has his cock buried inside me. I instinctively lash my legs around his hips.

Zane pumps into me hard and fast.

I bounce on his length while he holds me firmly with both hands and grunts with every inward lunge. Something about this bizarre position feels right. Even as I grow a bit dizzy, I keep begging him never to stop. While he grunts and growls and fucks me faster, I fling my arms above my head and give in to the freefall sensation. It's intoxicating. And the longer he takes me this way, the more I feel myself heading toward an orgasm that just might shatter me.

The world around me seems to vanish. All I see is him, all I feel is him inside me, and all I want is for this mind-altering experience to go on forever.

Weightless. Mindless. A slave to his passion. And I love it.

Zane pulls me up, plastering me to his body. He staggers backward until his calves bump into an obstacle. Only when he drops backward onto the mattress do I realize the bed was in his way. He doesn't need to say a word. I know what he wants, what he needs from me. I simply *know*. And I start to rock my hips, planting my hands on his chest while I ride him with abandon, not giving a toss what this ritual might be doing to me. Yes, I sense it is a ritual. But nothing else matters right now except our bodies merging.

I throw my had back, lost in the sensations.

Zane flips us over, hooking my leg over his shoulder, and pounds into me faster and harder than ever before. He repeats the same grunted word over and over. "Charlotte, Charlotte, Charlotte..."

He sets his hands on the bed at either side of my head.

I grasp his wrists, hanging on for the ride, however long it might last. When I wrap both my thighs around his hips, he pushes deeper inside me with every punishing thrust.

"Mine, Charlotte, mine."

"Yes, I am."

The orgasm that had been simmering inside me suddenly explodes, shattering me from the inside out. My inner muscles contract around his cock so forcefully that I can't breathe and my ears start to ring. The pleasure consumes me, too incredible to fight and perhaps too powerful even to survive. I feel as if I must have died. But I can hear the strangled roar that erupts from Zane, as well as the searing jet he unleashes inside me.

And I come again, screaming while I grow lightheaded.

Then darkness overtakes me.

Have I died? I detect sounds, but I can't figure out what they are. My senses have roused before the rest of me, though I can't force myself to open my eyes. Well, if I can still feel my eyelids, then I must not be dead. I remember that orgasm. It was body-shattering. The exhaustion I'd felt in the moment just before I passed out seems to have gone away. Rather than drained, I feel...languidly exhilarated. I suppose that doesn't make sense, but then, I had mind-altering sex with a demon. Sense has nothing to do with it.

A large, rough palm cups my face. "Are you awake, Charlotte?"

"Mm-hm." I still can't convince my eyes to open, but that's only because I feel so relaxed and satisfied. "Need another minute or two before I can get up."

"Take as long as you need."

Ambient sounds gradually penetrate my contented mind, but I can't make sense of them. Why would demons be playing the piano? And laughing? Why would I smell caramel? I also feel a cool breeze on my face. Those confusing realizations compel me to peel my lids open.

Zane sits on the bed's edge, gazing at me with concern.

I push up onto my elbows. "Where are we?"

"The Outlands. Don't you recognize this room? Or have I injured you so much that even your mind has shattered?"

Laughter bubbles out of me. "You are adorable when you're worried about me. That's not very demon-like. But to answer your question, I'm not injured at all. I didn't recognize where we were because I expected to wake up still inside your lair."

He whips the covers off me, exposing my nude body. "How do you feel?"

I stretch and sigh. "Very good."

"Then I've done it." He leans over me, grasping my chin with one hand. "You are mine forever, Lady Charlotte."

CHAPTER FIFTEEN

Zane

I STARE AT CHARLOTTE, STILL BAFFLED BY HER ATTITUDE. WHAT WE DID inside my lair was wild and carnal and dangerous for a mortal, but she seems unharmed. In fact, she appears happier than ever. How can this be? I abducted her, branded her as my mate, and she clearly knows that. But she almost seems to...like it.

Charlotte links her arms behind my nape. "I'm ravenous. Would you be a love and get me something to eat?"

"Yes, of course." I'm still leaning over her with our lips a hair's breadth apart. Her sweet smile and glittering gaze confound me. "I will go down to the saloon and have Lucy make up a plate of food for you."

"Thank you, Zane." She gives me a quick kiss. "I would also love a bath, if that's possible."

"I'll take care of that too."

She scans the room while keeping her arms around me. "How long was I asleep? Feels like no time at all."

"It was one hour and fourteen minutes."

"Since I don't see a clock anywhere in this room, how could you be so precise?"

Clearing my throat, I avert my gaze. "I counted the seconds and minutes in my mind. Demons generally have excellent recall."

"How fascinating. I would love to hear more about demons." She kisses me again. "Especially this demon."

I extricate myself from her embrace and slide off the bed. "You will find appropriate clothes on the chair. Get dressed while I fetch your meal and prepare a bath for you."

"Why should I bother getting dressed? I need a bath first."

"But it will take time to heat the water and bring the tub upstairs, then fill it. You might be chilled if you wait for that in the nude."

Dimples form in her cheeks. "You worry about me, don't you? That's very sweet, Zane."

Before she can speak again, I rush out of the room. Charlotte's kindness and understanding confuses me, considering what I did to her less than two hours ago. She should rail at me for abducting her. I've treated the girl with nothing but meanness. How can she call me sweet? The underworld, my home, is a place of violence, jealousy, anger, and hatred.

As I leap down the last three steps of the staircase, I catch sight of Lucy behind the bar. The patrons of this establishment scatter, desperate to get as far away from me as they can. Well, that at least proves they have a modicum of intellect, at least enough to protect their own skins.

Lucy lifts her brows when I halt in front of her. Only the bar itself separates us.

"I need food for Charlotte and a hot bath for her as well."

"Never heard the word please before have ya?"

I slam my fist down on the bar, making the glasses rattle. "Get me what I need, and get it now. Deny me and you will regret it."

The saloon harlot eyes me up and down, then grunts. "Lord Wolfie was a fair sight friendlier than you are, and that ain't sayin' much."

"Who is Lord Wolfie?"

"Nathaniel Fortescue, of course."

I despise hearing his name, and I can't disguise that fact. I slam my fist down on the bar again, but this time the whole room shudders. "Obey me, wench, or I will tear your throat out."

Charlotte's father is no longer a wolf, yet Lucy still refers to him that way. She probably hopes he will return to whisk her away and make her his mate. Yes, Lucy is that stupid.

The wench leans over the bar, deliberately giving me a view down her bodice. "Need a little more power, Zane? I fed your demon hunger real good last time."

Oh, yes, she is exactly as stupid as I believed. "Get the items I ordered. Now, Lucy, before I decide you are no longer of any use to me."

I let my eyes flame and whorl, just to ensure she will cease talking.

Lucy's face goes pale. She scurries away to gather what I need.

The patrons of this hellhole remain huddled on the other side of the room.

I lean against the bar, half-turned toward the patrons, and glare at them simply to prevent the morons from attempting to engage in conversation with me. They ought to know better. With these people, though, I can't guarantee they know anything.

Lucy returns, carrying a tray of food. "I'll get some of the boys to carry the tub upstairs while I heat the water."

I snatch the tray from her and march upstairs.

My footfalls pound on the steps, causing the whole staircase to shudder and probably the floor of the landing too. When I reach the bedroom, I hold the tray in one hand so I can open the door, swinging it wide.

Charlotte leaps off the bed, where she had been sitting with her legs dangling over the edge. "You're back. I thought it would take you longer."

"Did you assume I would take it slow just to torture you?"

"No. Why do you assume I would assume that?"

I set the tray on the bedside table. "Eat. Now."

"So, we're back to grumpy Zane." She rushes over to the table and lifts the metal lid that covers the food. A blissful smile curls her lips as she inhales the scents of her meal. "Oh, my word. The aromas are so sensual and enticing."

"Nothing about steak and potatoes is erotic. Gravy certainly isn't."

"You need to learn to appreciate the little things in life."

I grunt.

Charlotte laughs. "You're adorable, Zane."

She sits down on the bed, near the table, and rubs her hands together while humming with what I take for pleasure.

The girl must have been starving. Why else would she behave that way?

While she wolfs down her meal, I sit down on the chair opposite the table. I can't resist watching her eat, the way she consumes mashed potatoes as if they're an aphrodisiac. There isn't even any butter. At least now Charlotte wears clothing that won't awaken my demonic hunger for her body. Jeans and a loose-fitting plaid shirt seem unlikely to inflame my lust.

I gave her boots, yet her feet remain bare. "You are not fully clothed, Charlotte."

Her brows crinkle. "What?"

I point at her feet.

She laughs at me again. "My bare feet bother you? Well, feel free to suck on my toes if you like. I've heard some blokes like to do that, though I've never met that sort."

"Eat and be quiet."

"Your growly tone doesn't scare me." She stuffs a piece of steak into her mouth and gnaws on it with carnal satisfaction. "Mm, this is wonderful. Wouldn't you like to try some?"

"No."

She snatches up the glass of beer, the only type of liquid I could safely give her, and guzzles it. The water supply in the Outlands rates as well as that of any Wild West town in the normal world—meaning it's probably contaminated. I've seen men piss in the well. At least the beer in this establishment has a lower alcohol content than most. I only gave Charlotte a small glass, anyway.

"Do you eat, Zane?"

"Yes."

"But you don't eat with me. What foods do demons enjoy?"

"Anything we can kill." I slant toward her, lowering my voice. "That means you might be on the menu."

She rolls her eyes. "Please. You know better than to try that rubbish on me. I am not frightened of you, and I do not believe for one second that you would murder me and devour my remains."

"Your belief is irrelevant. Demons are carnivores."

"When was the last time you killed and ate a human being?"

I grind my teeth, blowing a breath out through my nostrils.

Charlotte smiles with smug satisfaction. "That's what I thought."

"What does that mean? I refused to answer your question."

"And that tells me everything I need to know." She spears a bite of meat, then holds it out to me. The fork hovers a hair's breadth from my lips. "Try a little steak, Zane. You might decide you like human food."

I pucker my lips.

She waves the fork in a spiraling motion. "Open up, Zane. Here comes the food train. Choo-choo, choo-choo."

"What are you doing? I am not a passenger on an invisible train."

Charlotte gives up waving the fork around, though she still holds it near my lips. And she sighs. "Mum did the choo-choo thing with Dad, here in this very room, and he liked it. I should've guessed you would be much less open to silliness."

I can't decide if she's insulting me, though I rather doubt it based on her sweet expression. Maybe that explains why I wrap my lips around the fork and pull the steak bite free. It lies on my tongue, warm and surprisingly tender. As I begin to chew, I note flavors I have never tasted before. I don't know how to describe them.

"You seem confused," Charlotte says. "I assume that's because this is your first time eating human food. You might notice the pepper, which is a sharper flavor. The meat itself tastes, well, meaty. There are hints of butter and salt too. I love steak that has garlic on it, but I guess the Outlands doesn't have that."

"What does garlic taste like?"

"Sweet, with a hint of spiciness. When garlic is ground up, it's very creamy."

When she offers me another bite, I consume it without hesitating. "What is your favorite food?"

"I adore fish and chips. You should know that, since you ate them too during our first date."

"Yes, I remember that now. Slabs of fried fish are very enticing, especially when one falls off your fork and makes a 'splat' sound."

She grins. "You made a joke, didn't you?"

I suppose I did, or at least I tried to do that. But I had little hope she would find my "joke" amusing. Yet now she's grinning at me. I don't understand why, so I need to be sure I'm interpreting her response correctly. "Never before have I been accused of attempting to be humorous, much less achieving that feat. Are you laughing at me for being a foolish bastard?"

"No, silly. I liked your joke."

"Why?"

"Because it was cute, and you looked so adorably relieved when I smiled. You aren't a soulless demon after all."

"All demons have souls."

Her brows hike up. "They do? I had no idea."

"Demonic souls aren't like the mortal version. They're crafted from pure evil."

"Then you must not be a demon at all, or at least not a full-blooded one. You've been kind to me often enough that I know you aren't evil." She thrusts a forkful of potatoes into her mouth and speaks while chewing. "I'm positive that your father is to blame for your attitudes about yourself."

Whatever she means by that statement, I don't want to know. Talking about my father is not something I like to do. I'd much rather listen to Charlotte telling me all about her family. They sound much more interesting than my kin.

Yet I intend to kill her parents. Don't I?

My plan to defile Charlotte and return her to her family in a pathetic, deranged condition seems to have…slipped my mind. Only for a while. Not very long at all.

She waves her hand in front of my face. "Earth to Zane. What frequency are you tuned into? Not the same one as I am, that's for sure."

"We are not on Earth. This is the Outlands."

"I know that." She consumes the last bite of her meal and wipes her mouth with the sleeve of her shirt. For a moment, she simply studies me. "The Outlands might be an alternate reality or something like that, but this place obeys the rules of the Wild West. Everyone dresses like that era. Yet you brought me modern clothes. Where did you get them?"

"Don't you feel more comfortable dressed this way?"

"Yes. But you haven't answered my question."

I scratch the back of my neck while wincing, though I had no conscious intention to do that. "Sex with you gave me more power, so I conjured some clothing."

"For me. Because you care about my happiness."

Her bald statement stuns me, and I find myself unable to speak or blink my eyes. They've begun to burn from the lack of moisture.

Charlotte shimmies closer to me. "Face it, Zane, you are not an evil, depraved demon. You're a decent man underneath all that growling and snarling and calling me insulting names."

"I apologize for my behavior."

We both stare blankly at each other. I can't believe I spoke those words. *I apologize.* It's hardly the first time I've said that to her, but it shocks me every time.

Charlotte kisses me.

No, it's more than a mere kiss. She presses her mouth to mine firmly, then softens her lips as she gazes into my eyes. What passes between us feels...intimate in ways I can't describe. More intimate than fucking her. When she slides her fingers up my throat to push them into my hair, my entire body relaxes.

Then someone bangs on the door. "Got yer tub, Zane. Do ya want us to bring it in now?"

"Yes, Cooper, please do."

Silence follows for precisely two seconds. Then, Cooper swings the door open. He, Ezra, and Jasper lug the metal tub into the room and attempt to set the ponderous thing down gently. But Jasper loses his grip, which causes the other two men to lose their grip as well. The tub hits the floor hard. Water sloshes but does not spill out.

I leap off the bed. "What are you morons doing? You were supposed to carry the tub up here while it was empty, then bring buckets of hot water to fill it with."

Cooper's entire face cinches up in a pained expression. "Sorry, Zane. It wasn't my idea to do it this way. Jasper and Ezra had the bright idea."

"It's a good thing this room has iron floors under the wood planks. You could have sent the tub crashing down into the saloon."

"We're real sorry," Ezra says. "Ain't never done nothing like this afore."

A growl resonates low in my throat. "Never mind. Leave us now."

The men exit, shutting the door behind them.

I approach the tub and dip my fingers into the water. "At least it's still warm enough, but not so hot that it might scald you."

"Still worrying about me, aren't you?"

I rise, turning toward Charlotte, and my breath catches. "You're naked."

Her gentle laughter tickles my senses. "Did you think I'd bathe with all my clothes on?"

"No. But—"

She steps into the tub and sits down. "Why don't you join me, Zane?"

CHAPTER SIXTEEN

Charlotte

I SWISH MY HANDS IN THE WARM WATER, LOVING THE FEEL OF IT, and can't stop myself from moaning with pleasure. When was the last time I had a real bath? Our dip in the pool beside the Kevitash butte was lovely, but the water was lukewarm at best. Zane brought me a hot bath. "Mm, this is delicious. Please join me."

"Not enough room. All the water would splash out."

I sink down into the blessedly warm water and let it rinse my hair out. When I rise from the water again, Zane is looking at me through slitted eyes and licking his lips. Oh, I recognize that expression. He wants to shag me. As much as I would love that, I still feel a touch sore after our bonding ritual in the underworld. So, instead of letting him seduce me, I choose the less exhausting but also less fun option.

"Come on, Zane, join me in the tub. I could sit on your lap, then there would be plenty of room for both of us. You need to relax. Baths are wonderful for that."

"I told you the water will splash out."

"Who cares?" I raise my arms above my head, close my eyes halfway, and moan. The hot water feels so bloody good. "You know you want to get in this tub with me."

"Yes, I do." His voice has become gruffer and deeper. His gaze travels over me from head to toe while he licks his lips repeatedly. "Have it your way."

He literally rips his clothes off, probably shredding it so thoroughly that I doubt it could be repaired. Then he steps into the tub. "Bend your knees. I won't fit otherwise."

I draw my knees up to my chest, watching while he sinks into the water inch by inch as if he's unsure of how to get into a bathtub. I love watching that outrageously muscular body sliding down ever-so-slowly. Even moving at such a slow pace, he displaces enough water that at least a bucketful spills onto the floor. I watch the water spreading out on the wood planks, but they won't get past the iron floor.

Zane draws his knees up, though not all the way to his massive chest. He casually settles his wrists on his knees. "Happy now, sweet little Charlotte?"

He used to call me that with a nasty tone in his voice. Now, he speaks it in a gentle and almost affectionate manner.

Zane spreads his thighs. "Come closer. You need to be sitting on my lap."

"Do I?"

"We both know it's where you want to be, cradled between my thighs with my cock nestled against your backside."

He's already hard. I'm beginning to think that's his normal state. Are all demons this randy? All I care about is this demon, so I follow his command, rising to my knees, waddling closer until I reach his bent legs. Then I shuffle around and settle in between his powerful thighs. I do indeed feel his erection pressed up against my lower back. As I lean my head against his chest, he stretches his legs out as much as he can. I do the same, though the tub is long enough for me to extend my legs fully. He can't do that.

Zane begins to comb his fingers through my hair in a soothing rhythm. "Do you like this?"

"I love it. You give the best scalp massages." As much as I do love this new intimacy between us, I need to get back to the questions I'd meant to ask him. "You mentioned you used to be the general of the demon army. That must mean you were once a powerful man in the underworld."

He grunts. "Hardly. The army is necessary, but no one reveres us. We are the lowest of the low in the underworld."

"But in the land of humans, most people at least appreciate the men and women who serve in the military. Many of us value them highly and take every chance to express our appreciation."

"Mortals are far more forgiving than demons." He keeps massaging my scalp but also begins to run his rough palm gently up and down my arm. "An army exists to wage war. The demon hordes love bloodshed. Only the worst elements of our society, such as it, will be conscripted into the collective armies. Convincing demons from different clans to behave is a dangerous job."

"But you did that. If Rahn'omith let you stay on as general, he must have realized you have skills he needed."

"The usurper king kept me as general strictly to torment me—until he grew tired of that." He wraps his arm around me. "In the armies of the demon hordes, everyone is constantly trying to seize the rank of general by any means necessary. I have suffered grievous injuries at the hands of my underlings more times than I can count."

"Let's not talk about that anymore. I can tell it upsets you." I reach behind my head to touch his cheek. "Let's just enjoy this little respite for a while."

He kisses my palm. "Anything for you, sweet Charlotte."

A crack of thunder detonates overhead with such force that the building shakes.

I spring upright. "What was that? Sounded like thunder, but I don't think it was."

"Nothing in the Outlands is anything like the mortal-world version."

He hugs me tightly and stands up, taking me with him. Then he sets me on my feet on the cold wood floor. "Something is wrong. Get dressed. Now."

A thread of anxiety tightens his voice. Zane anxious? That is not a good sign. He pulls his trousers on, the only element of his outfit that he didn't shred a few minutes ago.

I struggle to get my clothes on while I'm still wet from head to toe, but I accomplish the task faster than I thought I could under the circumstances. I can feel something in the air, though I can't describe the sensation. It's almost like static electricity.

Zane gets his boots on before I can finish tying my shoes.

He yanks the door open and glances at me over his shoulder. "Remain here. I need to go outside to...check on things."

"Wait. I should go with—"

Zane rushes out the door and slams it shut behind him.

I stumble and almost fall down but finally manage to get my shoes on. As I rip the door open, rushing down the hall, a series of even louder explosions detonate above my head—in the sky, I'm certain. This time, I see the flashes of light. At the top of the staircase, I jump onto the bannister and slide down it to reach the saloon floor as quickly as possible.

But I don't see Zane.

I race to the bar, where Lucy stands frozen with her eyes wide and her lips trembling. The patrons are scrambling to escape from the building, as if they believe being outdoors will protect them. "Lucy, where did Zane go?"

She just stands there wide-eyed, as if she's entranced.

I reach across the bar to seize her arms and give her a violent shake. "Where did Zane go?"

Lucy blinks rapidly, then looks at me. "No idea. He skedaddled like he had fire-breathing dragons on his tail."

"Which direction did he go when he left the saloon?"

She points a shaking arm.

And I sprint outside, leaping down the steps and onto the dirt road. Swerving left, the direction Lucy had indicated, I run faster than I ever have before. Every footfall slaps on the ground, and my pulse pounds in my ears. Every hair at my nape shivers erect. Then I see Zane. He stands in the center of the road, shoulders bunched, fists clenched, bathed in the reddish glow that emanates from the sky. Past him stand several humanoid shapes. I can't quite make them out.

Zane swings his head around to glower at me. "Stop right there, you stupid little girl."

That's fear in his voice. I'm sure of it.

I stop dead. What should I do now? Run back into the saloon? I doubt that will spare me from whatever those demons mean to do next. I march up to Zane, halting right beside him. He glowers at me again, but his lips tick up slightly for half a second, and I know that means he isn't genuinely angry with me.

No, he's as frightened as I am.

Now I can see the six demons that stand on the street no more than twenty feet away. They all appear to be as nasty as any creature could get. Two have saliva dribbling from their lips as if they can't wait to devour a few humans.

The loudest explosion yet detonates directly above our heads. The ground shudders as if an earthquake has occurred. I stumble into Zane, but he doesn't move even one millimeter. The flash of light that follows the explosion blinds me briefly, then everything inside me goes cold.

A demon stands a few yards away, smirking and chuckling. "You knew you couldn't escape me for long, Zaen'imuth. Your reckoning has come."

Zane blusters a breath out through his nostrils. "The usurper will be the one to fall, Rahn'omith."

"You will call me Your Majesty."

Zane grits his teeth and snarls, "You are not the rightful king, and I will no longer countenance your treachery. You have stolen the throne from me, but I will give you one last chance to concede the title and bow down before me."

I doubt Zane actually wants to take the throne and rule the underworld. He must have an idea for getting us out of this mess. I need to trust that he knows what he's doing. Annoying a powerful demon who has an army behind him, literally, wouldn't be a clever plan. But Zane is clever.

Figures move about in the shadows that surround the buildings. Those must be the men and women who were consigned to this town, though some of them would be the tourists who got swept up in the spell cast by the Rom witch Kezia. People will die tonight, that seems inevitable. I pray only the bad ones, like the men who inhabit the saloon, will suffer that fate.

Rahn'omith cracks his knuckles and grins with feral hunger. "If those are your terms, then we will do battle. There is no other option for you"—He rakes his gaze over my body.—"though perhaps I'll spare the girl. She would make an excellent concubine."

"You will never touch her because I will rip you apart before you can get within spitting distance of Charlotte."

Spittle sprayed from Zane's lips when he spoke those words, and I know he meant every syllable. He will rend the flesh from every demon to protect me. I feel a strangely warm shiver sidling up my spine as I realize that Zane would do anything to protect me. *Anything.*

Rahn'omith conjures a sword, a wicked one with a serrated blade and strange symbols etched into the metal. He twirls the sword in a showy attempt to seem...cool? I don't know, but whatever his aim is, it doesn't impress my demon. Zane curls the fingers of one hand loosely, almost as if he were holding a sword too.

The usurper laughs. "Did you think I would allow you to retain your magics during our battle? That would make me incredibly stupid."

Zane tenses, preparing for a fight. But he only has his body to use as a weapon while Rahn'omith and his army wield wicked-looking blades and maces.

I need to do something. What? I have no sodding clue.

Mum used magics to destroy Zor'imuth. She wasn't a witch or any sort of paranormal being. Yet she possessed those powers because of her love for Dad and their sensual connection. Mum told me that once, though she left out the details. I never wanted to hear about those bits of the story. Yet now, I wish I had asked her to tell me everything.

Does shagging a paranormal being invest a person with power? It must. How else could Mum have stopped the former demon king? It had something to do with the Kevitash butte and the chamber inside it. Zane and I went there together. So, that might mean...

Rahn'omith veers his attention to me. He narrows his gaze, and I get the unsettling feeling that he's sizing me up. The demon king thrusts his blade toward Zane, but he keeps his gaze on me.

And he shouts, "Seize the girl!"

Oh, bollocks. He must have figured out that I might possess magics. Maybe it showed on my face when I realized the truth.

Zane takes two seconds too long to grasp the situation, and the demon king's minions move much faster. Before I can even try to run, the slavering cretins have me in their grasp. I can't believe they think they need two demons to control me, but that only proves what I'd thought. I must have powers inside me, if only I could figure out how to access them.

Rahn'omith grins at Zane. "I have your girl. And now, it's time to end you forever."

The usurper thrusts his blade toward Zane, who jumps sideways to avoid the sword. Rahn'omith shouts to his minions in what I take for the demon language. Several demons race toward Zane. He sees the one in front of him, but he doesn't know about the ones that have materialized behind him.

"Zane! Watch out, they're behind you!"

He hurls his body sideways again. But this time, he trips and hits the ground, rolling toward the porch of the saloon.

Magics, now would be a good time to kick in, please. Despite my call to whatever unknown powers reside in the Outlands, nothing happens. I don't feel any different. I've been struggling to break free of my captors, though I have zero chance of defeating the huge creatures. Instead of fighting, I exhale and relax every muscle, every sinew, until I've gone limp.

Rahn'omith has just raced toward Zane, but he stops when he notices my limp body. "What is wrong with you, child?"

I let my head sag backward and moan as if I'm exhausted and on the verge of death.

The crown stealer strides over to me, where I hang with only the arms of the two demons to hold me upright. "What have you morons done to her? She was to remain intact until I can take her to my lair."

"Sorry to disappoint you," I say, slurring my voice a touch on purpose. "The stress is too much for a waif like me."

Zane still sits on the ground, held up with one straight arm. He knows better than to speak right now.

I have my opening. I snap my head forward, stand on my own two feet, and fling my palms out as I command my powers to obey me.

And a stream of glittering gold magics erupts from my palms.

CHAPTER SEVENTEEN

Zane

I LEAP TO MY FEET, READY TO RUSH OVER THERE AND SAVE CHARlotte. But she doesn't seem to need saving. I can't figure out what she's doing or how she's doing it, though I'm not stupid enough to get close to her or the demons who are caught in her magics. When did sweet little Charlotte develop supernatural powers?

Maybe I've underestimated her. No, not maybe. I have definitely done that.

Rahn'omith reaches out to grab Charlotte, only to be scalded by her magics. The two demons who had seized her now regret it intensely, I'm sure. The shimmering golden energy is melting the flesh from their hands. One of them pulls away just in time to save his arms. The other seems too stunned to move. Charlotte takes pity on that poor bastard, shaking his hands free to spare him from total destruction.

At least half of the small army the usurper had brought with him have fled the Outlands by teleporting or simply running away. The two Charlotte had injured are racing away as fast as they can, disappearing into the night.

Charlotte stands alone in the center of the street.

I hurry over to her. "Are you injured?"

She shakes her head slowly. "Are you all right?"

"Yes." I glance back at Rahn'omith, who remains immobilized where he'd stood a second before Charlotte invoked her magics. "The usurper seems confused."

"He would be. I am too." She rubs her arms as if she's cold. "Not sure what I did or how I did it. I wanted to destroy Rahn'omith, but it wasn't as easy as it sounded. Mum didn't have this much trouble dispatching a demon, from what she told me."

I catch a scent in the air, and my senses shift into high gear. "Something worse than Rahn'omith is coming. We must go. Now."

"What about these innocent people? And the not-so-innocent ones? They're human beings, and they're trapped here."

I glance around, noting the human shapes that hide within the shadows. "What would you have me do? I can't teleport them all away. Defeating the usurper has proved much more difficult than I expected."

"Can't you steal his power the way he stole your throne?"

She makes that sound like a simple task. "Your mother is the only mortal I know of who could take down a demon king."

"But you are the rightful king. Take back your crown."

The fact that demons don't wear actual crowns has no bearing on the situation, so I'll keep that information to myself. Maybe I can do what she suggested.

Charlotte's eyes go wide as she stares at something past my shoulder.

I turn around—and watch Rahn'omith barreling toward us. I haul Charlotte into my arms and teleport us to the other end of town.

The usurper appears directly in front of us, grinning like a deranged animal. "My men have surrounded the town and the Kevitash butte. You cannot escape. Give in and pledge your fealty to me, then perhaps I won't kill you."

I chuckle with no humor at all. "You will murder us either way, so we might as well fight you with everything we have."

"And that is...what, exactly?" His mouth stretches into a gleeful sneer. "Oh, that's right. Everything you have is precisely nothing."

I wish I hadn't used up all the extra magics I'd gathered when I escaped from the underworld and when I summoned the sorceress. I squandered it on a useless quest to exact revenge on Kylie and Nathaniel and to drag their daughter into hell. Still, I can't regret the path I chose. It brought me to Charlotte.

And I will do anything, even sacrifice my own life, to save her.

If only I had a plan...

The scent I'd detected earlier wafts over me again, stronger this time. What is it? If I could identify the smell, I might know whether it could help me.

Rahn'omith reaches for Charlotte.

I punch him in the gut hard enough to send him flying backward. He slams down flat on his backside, creating a usurper-shaped depression. "Never touch her again, you fucking bastard. You should have known better than to confront me alone. Or maybe your minions have abandoned you."

"No one would dare defy me."

Charlotte nods toward me. "Oh, you mean the way Zane has done? Seems like it's bloody easy to get away from you."

A silence deeper than death drops down on us. I feel it almost as a palpable weight, and the scent I detected earlier returns, more prominently than before.

Something is coming.

No, that's wrong. Something *has* come. What it wants, what it will do, remains unknowable.

Even Rahn'omith freezes and moves only his eyes to scan the vicinity. His nostrils flare as he tests the atmosphere as I'd done a moment ago.

The residents of the Outlands emerge from their hiding places, milling around in the street, clearly affected by the change in the atmosphere and in the magics that should be everywhere around us. But a strange new phenomenon has taken hold of the town—and the butte. The ones who had long ago been condemned to this place now move among the average mortals who had been swept up in the tempest when Charlotte and I arrived here.

"What have you done, Zaen'imuth?" the false king snarls. "How you acquired such powerful magics, I cannot comprehend. But you won't keep them for long. Release the spell you've invoked. Do it now."

He believes I have done this to the Outlands. I haven't, but perhaps I can milk his misconception, for a moment, at least. "I vowed you would never take Charlotte from me. Did you think I'd lie down and let you rub my belly?"

Rahn'omith raises his hand, curling the fingers as if he wants to pick up an object. He flexes his fingers and waits. He flexes them three more times, to no avail. The moron growls and tries again, with no better luck. "Where is my sword? You've done something with it, haven't you, Zaen'imuth?"

The air pressure seems to be increasing little by little. Charlotte is breathing harder, and even I begin to feel the effects. No more games. I must take action now and cut the head off the snake. I clasp Charlotte's hand, praying the physical contact will combine our magics.

The usurper tries once again to conjure a sword, with no better results.

But I don't feel my powers expanding. Damn the magics, they won't help me at all. But when I glance at Charlotte, she looks at me too, and a different sort of power zings between us. That's when I realize what I need to do.

I drag Charlotte into my arms and kiss her.

Energies I have never felt before rush through my veins and infiltrate my flesh from the surface down deep into my body and my soul. I thrust my tongue between her lips, coiling it round and round like an agile serpent until she sags into me and moans softly. Charlotte throws her arms around my neck, lifting herself onto her toes while he devour each other as if the world is ending.

It might be ending—unless my idea works.

The hairs all over my body rise and stiffen, triggering a tingle that heightens my lust for this woman. No, it's more than lust now. Charlotte has become a part of me, and I am now a part of her. Without speaking, without even giving up each other's lips, we send out threads of magic. They encircle every human being in this town, shielding them from what will come at any moment.

Apocalypse. That's what is coming for the Outlands now.

Rahn'omith screams.

I peel one lid open to see what's going on. The usurper is...folding in on himself while his skin begins to melt. His scream turns into a wet choking sound. His minions are also melting, and soon enough, they become red puddles on the ground. Charlotte and I stare at the ground as the remains of the usurper and his minions bleed into the earth and vanish as if they had never existed.

The silence that fills the void feels uncanny.

I hold Charlotte close. All we can do is wait for what comes next.

A breeze tickles our faces. Little by little, the wind grows stronger until it becomes a gale. I cover Charlotte's face with my hand to protect her and squeeze my own eyes shut. The dust swirling up into the gale threatens to blind us.

Suddenly, the wind vanishes.

I peel my lids open, but I can't understand what I'm seeing.

Charlotte hugs me tightly. "What is that?"

All I can do is shake my head. Before us hover writhing shadows that seem to have a vaguely human form. Their eyes glow the purest white I've ever seen.

I push Charlotte behind me. "Who are you? What do you want?"

A dark figure separates from the writhing shadows to halt in front of us.

I stare at the figure. "Kezia?"

Her form shimmers and coalesces into a solid state. I had recognized her from her facial features, but now I can see her entire body. "Yes, Zaen'imuth, I have returned."

"To destroy me. That's what you've wanted all along."

She cants her head to the side, studying me. "I was wrong about you, Zane. You are not a carbon copy of your father, and your journeys have changed you. For the better, I believe. That is why we have come to you now."

"We?" I skim my gaze over the writhing shadow figures. "I don't understand any of this or what you intend to do now. Who are those beings behind you?"

Kezia spreads her arms wide. "We are the Kevitash."

Her voice booms through the Outlands, echoing off buildings and the butte too, I'm certain.

"But you are of the Rom," I point out. "Those people come from Europe. The Kevitash are a tribe native to this region in Utah, though they have long since been eradicated due to Erosabel's curse."

"All will become clear soon." She moves closer, now standing an arm's length from me. "We expected this to end with your death. But Charlotte has reformed you, and we longer wish for you to be destroyed."

"Why not? I was an evil bastard for most of my life."

Charlotte ducks under my arm, wrapping hers around me. She gazes up at me with an expression I can only describe as...loving. As if I know anything about such feelings. "You aren't a villain, Zane. No one who is truly evil could treat me with kindness and tenderness, and someone like that would never worry about the lives of strangers. You've done all of those things."

My throat feels thick, and my eyes begin to sting. Whatever is happening to me, I have no frame of reference for it. Demons do not experience such things.

Kezia moves closer to us. "Zaen'imuth, son of the demon king, the choice is yours and yours alone. Do you wish to claim the throne that is rightfully yours? Or would prefer a different path, one that includes Charlotte? A mortal cannot survive in the underworld."

For a moment, I stand perfectly still with my gaze aimed at the Rom witch. Then words tumble from my lips, though I had no conscious desire to speak. "I can no longer see my life without Charlotte. The throne means nothing to me, but she means everything. I do not want to rule the underworld."

Charlotte curls her fingers into my chest. "What will happen to you now?"

"Kezia has given me a choice. Now, she must explain the consequences of my decision." I face the Rom witch. "Answer Charlotte's question, please."

She lifts her chin, gazing at me steadily. "You must become human. The process will be painful, but it is the only way."

"Do it."

Kezia turns her attention to Charlotte. "Stand back, child. The magics required to complete this task are volatile and tortuous." The witch faces me. "Are you certain this is what you want?"

"I will submit myself to any torment if it means I can be with Charlotte."

The Rom witch waves her arms in a grand gesture. "Clear the area! This will be a perilous task, and my people do not wish for any of you to be harmed." She squints at the area beyond where Charlotte and I stand. "Further away! You are still too close. Ah, that's it. You should be safe there." Kezia takes hold of Charlotte's wrist. "Come, child, you must back away as well. You may remain with me, but you must do exactly as I tell you."

"I understand."

Charlotte and Kezia trot a considerable distance away, though not as far as the Rom witch had told the townspeople to go. I can't hear it when she speaks to Charlotte, and I've never been a skilled lip-reader. Then Charlotte nods and produces the Kevitash medallion from her pocket. Kezia encourages her to drape the medallion and its chain around her neck so that the bronze disk lies directly over her breastbone.

Kezia tips her head back and spreads her arms. Then she chants in a language I don't recognize, though I assume it's the tongue of the Kevitash or the Rom, perhaps a combination of both. It's certainly not the demon language. More voices join in the chanting, the sound seeming to originate from sky.

Shadowy figures writhe overhead, high above the tallest building in the Outlands. Sparks of red, white, and orange rain down, but they sputter out before they can touch Kezia, Charlotte, or anyone else in this town.

But they do land on my skin, scalding my body. With every passing second, the sparks grow larger and hotter. They melt my flesh, just as the Kevitash medallion had once done, but I grit my teeth and keep my gaze nailed to Charlotte, refusing to let her see how much pain I'm enduring. The rain of sparks explodes into a deluge, and at last, I cannot disguise the torment the spell is causing.

I fall to my knees, roaring in agony.

My flesh has become a viscous puddle on the ground, exposing my bones. As my skeleton begins to crumble away, the agony erases me at last. Darkness envelops me in a blanket of silence. The pain has vanished.

Am I dead?

I don't think so, since I can feel the weight of my body pressing down on the cool earth. I smell it too as I realize I can breathe again.

"Zane!" Charlotte cries out. Footsteps echo from elsewhere, drawing closer. A hand touches my head. "Zane, can you open your eyes?"

I groan.

Another set of footfalls approach from the other side of my body. "He is alive, child, and will remain so until the day of his natural death arrives. We have done our part. His fate lies in his own hands now. Goodbye, Charlotte Fortescue and Zaen'imith."

Charlotte slaps my cheek. "Wake up, Zane. It's all over. Or do you mean to sleep until the sun comes up?"

CHAPTER EIGHTEEN

Charlotte

ZANE SPLAYS HIS PALMS ON THE EARTH AND HEAVES HIMSELF UP AND onto all fours. Then he glances around as if he doesn't recognize me or the town. He scratches the back of his neck, twisting his mouth into a slightly annoyed expression. "That wasn't the greeting I expected. I thought you'd be happier to see me alive."

"Of course I'm happy. Ecstatic, actually." I fling my arms around him. "Now get up off your arse. I need to kiss you."

Zane slings an arm around me and leaps to his feet. "Did you say something about kissing me?"

I grin, feeling a joy like nothing I've ever experienced before. "Yes, I mean to kiss you until we're both breathless. But you're so bloody tall that I can't reach your lips without a bit of help."

He hoists me off the ground. "Our lips are aligned now. Go on and kiss me."

With my feet dangling in the air, I crush my mouth to his, wasting not even one second before I plunge my tongue between his lips. Zane lets me take command of the kiss. I need to join with him in every way possible, but we can't shag until we're alone. So, I settle for devouring the flavor of his mouth and feeling the way our tongues tangle until I can't tell who's doing what.

His cock is growing harder by the second.

When we finally disentangle, Zane sets me down on my feet and brushes a lock of hair away from my face. "Letting you be in control of that kiss was the sweetest torture any male of any species could hope to feel. You consumed me as if you never wanted to stop."

"I could kiss you forever."

Zane pulls me close, just to hold me. I rest my cheek on his chest and listen to the rhythm of his heartbeats. I feared I might lose him, but I should have known better. Zaen'imuth would never let that happen.

"Are you two done bussin'?" a familiar voice asks. "Some of us wanna know what in tarnation that gypsy did to you."

Zane lifts me just high enough that he can spin around with me in his arms. The joy on his face infects me too. "Stop shouting, Lucy. We will explain everything later. Right now, Charlotte and I have things to discuss."

Lucy starts to complain, but Zane squints at her. And she shuts her mouth.

The lighting is rather dim out here, and I can't yet tell in what manner the Kevitash spell has changed him. I don't need to wait long, though. Zane sweeps me up into his arms and marches down the street, veering toward the saloon. He mounts the steps in one stride, then stalks through the doors. The entire town had been plunged into darkness, but now, the lights come on inside the saloon all on their own. As the doors swing shut, I get a glimpse of lights flickering to life throughout the town.

Zane takes the stairs four at a time. The building shudders faintly.

We reach the ironclad bedroom in a few seconds. I twist the knob and shove the door open. Zane marches inside, kicking the door shut.

Then he drops me onto the bed. "Strip, Charlotte."

"You first. I need to see all of the new you."

He freezes in the middle of unbuttoning his trousers. "New me?"

"Don't like being a new man? It was a compliment, love."

Zane removes his shoes and kicks his trousers away, now gloriously nude. "If you don't like that I'm now a man—"

I kneel in front of him and seal his lips with one finger. "Hush, darling. I love you, no matter what you are."

"But I can no longer protect you from supernatural threats, and sex with me won't be the same as it had been when I was a demon." He freezes again, and his eyes nearly bulge out of their sockets. "What did you just say?"

"That I want you no matter what sort of man you are."

"No, you said—But you couldn't have meant it."

I clasp his hands, holding them to my chest, to my heart. "Please tell me what's wrong, Zane. What did I say that upset you?"

He gazes into my eyes with the sweetest look of longing. "You said you love me. But you must have not have meant it the way it sounded."

"Of course I did. I meant every syllable." I lean forward to touch my lips to his. "I love you, Zane. Or would you rather be called Zaen'imith?"

"I am not Zaen'imuth any longer because I am not a demon." He cups my face in his hand, peering into my eyes once again. "I love you, Charlotte."

"Good. Then I won't need to whack you over the head with a blunt object and shackle you to this bed." I run my tongue across his bottom lip. "This time when we make love, I'd like to be on top. How do you feel about that?"

"I still haven't recovered from what you said. You love me."

He spoke those words as if he couldn't quite believe they're true. Zane has never known real love, not from his father or from any of his fellow demons. It will take time for him to feel human, despite becoming a mortal.

I start unbuttoning my shirt. "Yes, I love you. That will never change."

"What about your family? They can't accept me."

"Don't worry about Mum and Dad. They love me and trust me, so they'll get used to me being with a former demon." I've removed all my clothes, which means it's time to change the topic of conversation. "All I want to hear you say for the next hour is filthy things. Lie down on your back, Zane. Let me be in command."

He climbs onto the bed and lies down on his back. His old self-confidence returns, evidenced by his sexy smirk and the way he clasps his hands under his head. His erection waves like a flag, beckoning me.

I kneel at his feet, then slide my hands up and down his legs. "Do you remember that thing I wanted to do to you on the night we first shagged?"

Zane scrunches up his face as if he's trying to recall that night. Then his mouth slides into a sexy grin. "Do whatever you like, sweet Charlotte. I'm yours forever."

I lie down between his thighs, setting my hands on his hips. "Can't wait to devour you, Zane, and taste you."

"Don't make me come. I need to do that while I'm inside you."

"It's a deal."

Zane relaxes, and he groans with deep satisfaction as if he loves having me do this to him. And I haven't even begun yet.

His erection waves, though it doesn't stand up ramrod straight the way it had when he was a demon. I prefer this version of him, including all his imperfections. I'm not perfect either. That's what being human is all about.

When I bend my head, my hair falls over his cock.

Zane hisses in a sharp breath. "I never used to be this sensitive."

"You're a man now. Your body has changed. Is this too much for you?"

"No, keep going." He smirks. "But if you want me to come inside you, better not drape your silky hair over my erection."

"Sorry. I didn't mean to do that."

I pull my hair back and tie it in a knot using my own hair as a scrunchy. Then I lower my head again and kiss the crown of his cock. Zane groans deeply. I know he likes what I did because his eyes drift partly closed. He watches me with a sensual little smile on his lips while I grasp the base of his erection and pump it slowly. I keep my gaze on him, while he keeps his on me. When I finally take him into my mouth, he groans again with even more contentment.

Mm, yes, the salty taste of him gets me even randier. I lick and suckle his cock while pumping him with my hand, growing so aroused that I start making ravenous noises that don't sound like me at all.

Zane bends his knees, hoisting his hips every time I slide my hand upward. "Almost there already. Please, Charlotte, I need to come inside your body."

"Don't worry, we'll do that." Now that I've pulled my mouth free, I massage his inner thighs with both hands. "I love the flavor of you, and the next time we shag, I need to swallow everything you have."

"Ride me now, baby, or I'll flip us over and do it myself."

He has never called me "baby" before, but I like it.

And I take pity on him. Rising onto my knees, I waddle into position and grasp his erection. Then I guide his length inside me inch by delicious inch until he's seated deep inside me. Once I begin to rock my hips, I can't hold back anymore. "Oh, God, Zane, I'm already on the edge."

"I am too, so fuck me hard, baby." His growled statement makes me shiver with delight.

Leaning forward, I plant my hands on his chest and buck my hips wildly, like a crazed cowgirl. My tits bounce wildly too, and Zane fists his hands in the sheets while gritting his teeth. We both need to climax. I realize that, but I can't stop myself from riding him with abandon.

Zane suddenly thrusts his hips up.

And I come. The orgasm rips through me with such power that I lose my breath. All my inner muscles clamp down on him, and I know he won't last much longer either. I cry out and dig my nails into his skin. Zane flips us over and pounds into me a few times while my climax finally wanes.

He drops onto his back on the bed.

I roll onto my side to cuddle up to him. "Wow, Zane, sex with the human you isn't any less incredible than when you were a demon. You are awesome."

His lips curve into a lopsided smirk. "So are you, sweet Charlotte."

"Mm, I love being with you, sweet Zane."

"Please don't call me that in front of anyone else."

A laugh tumbles out of me. "But you are sweet. And once my parents meet you and see the real Zane, they'll agree." I push up onto one elbow. "Are you giving up your demon name? Or will you still officially be Zaen'imuth?"

"That is the name given to me by my father. I don't care to keep it." He slides an arm around me. "From now on, I am only Zane."

"Well, in the human world, you'll need a surname. Oh, and some sort of history to explain where you came from."

"How do I acquire a 'history'?"

"To sort that out, we'll need to go back to the mundane world, I think."

Zane shuts his eyes and groans. "How will we do that? I have no powers anymore. Do you?"

"Not sure. Let's get dressed and try to find out. Maybe the Kevitash can help us." I sit up, biting my lip as I consider the issues ahead of us. "My parents might know what to do. Maybe we should go to Wilderhampton first."

Zane springs upright, his eyes wide. "We can't go there. Your parents will want to murder me, and they have every right to do it."

"No, they do not. You aren't a demon anymore. And I will testify to what a wonderful man you've become."

His shock lingers, though it lessens a bit. "I doubt they will be as understanding as you are."

"Give them a chance to get to know you. Mum and Dad are good people. I adore them to bits, and I'm certain they'll see why I adore you to bits too."

Zane still seems rather unconvinced, but he doesn't know Lord and Lady Wilderhampton the way I do.

As we walk down the stairs into the saloon, everyone watches us with slight trepidation. They might know that Zane is now human, but they also remember the rampaging demon he used to be. He never hurt anyone who didn't deserve it, but I understand why the townsfolk are uncertain of him.

Lucy greets us, and she studies my boyfriend as if she's never seen Zane before. The sun has risen in the Outlands. That means everyone is getting their first good look at the former demon. He does look different, but that's mostly because his skin is much paler and his eyes are a deep brown instead of that eerie reddish-brown col-

or. His muscles have shrunk just a bit. He looks like an average bodybuilder now.

Of course, he still towers over everyone.

Lucy's lips gradually curve into a smile. "You look darn good this way, Zane. Will you be our new sheriff?"

"No. I can't. I, ah, don't have the qualifications."

"You know all about the underworld and them demons. Besides, you're one tough cuss."

I grasp Zane's hand. "Don't rush him, Lucy. Zane just went through an intense transition. He's coming home with me now, but we'll let you know when and if he decides to take over the sheriff's position."

When I glance up at Zane, his stunned expression has reasserted itself.

I pat his chest. "Relax, love, no one expects you to live in the Outlands. Please, let me show you Wilderhampton. Once you've met my parents and they've gotten used to you, only then will we discuss what Lucy suggested."

"All right. But how do we get to your home? I have no magics."

Oh, I'm not convinced that's true. No longer being a demon doesn't mean he's lost all his supernatural powers. But we can talk about that later. Much later. First, we need to jump that hurdle and introduce my new boyfriend to Mum and Dad. Yes, my former-werewolf father and my strong-willed mother will, I'm sure, give my former-demon lover a pleasant welcome.

Blimey. What have I gotten myself into this time?

"Oh!" I exclaim, hunting about for a certain item. "How could I have forgotten? I still have the Kevitash medallion. That will take us home."

Zane reaches inside my blouse to pluck up the medallion. "How does it work?"

I bat his hand away. "We'll need to do something about your manners. You still act like a ruddy demon sometimes."

"Maybe you can teach me how to behave like a human."

"For you, I will do anything."

He flattens his lips as he studies my chest.

I raise my brows. "Lesson one. Staring at a woman's cleavage is rude, Zane."

"But I love your tits." He rubs his jaw and wrenches his gaze away from my chest. "I wasn't staring at your cleavage, though. Not entirely, that is. I wondered if I can touch the medallion now without melting my skin."

"Only one way to know. Go on, try it."

CHAPTER NINETEEN

Zane

MY GAZE FLICKS DOWN TO THE MEDALLION, AND SUDDENLY, I DON'T feel at all certain about doing this. Having my flesh melt was not a pleasant experience the first time, and I don't relish feeling that way again. I suggested maybe I should try again. I can't very well back out now. I would seem like a weak, frightened mortal if I did.

I grasp the back of my neck and wince. "All right. Give me the medallion."

Charlotte removes it from her neck and hands me the thing. "If you feel even a twinge of melti-ness, drop the medallion immediately."

"Is melti-ness a word? It doesn't sound like one."

She bumps her hip into me. "Cheeky sod."

Whatever that means, it sounds like a compliment when she speaks the words.

Time to bite the bullet—or the bronze disk, as the case may be. I hold the medallion by its chain and move away from Charlotte and Lucy. No one else had approached us when we emerged from the ironclad room, so I don't need to worry about them.

When the women stop walking, I wave for them to go further away. They both roll their eyes at me, but they do what I suggested.

Standing here on the street, in the sunshine, I feel a new and strange sensation. The sun warms my skin, and its light blinds me when I look straight at it. How strange. I push aside those thoughts and focus on my task. Holding a medallion in my hand shouldn't cause me anxiety. I remember vividly the moment when Charlotte handed it to me and my skin began to dissolve, and I don't relish going through that again. I was a damn demon for more millennia than I care to count. This task is nothing compared to that torture.

I pull in a deep breath and hold it as I drop the medallion onto my palm.

No pain. No melting. So far, I'm unharmed.

Then I wrap my fingers around the medallion and wait for the agony to begin. Yet again, I experience no agony. Not a twinge. Absolutely nothing. I slap the thing onto my cheek, and still I do not melt or burst into flames.

Charlotte races up to me. "You aren't melting." She kisses my cheek and grins. "You know what that means."

"I won't be a puddle of congealed flesh."

"No, silly. It means the Kevitash have accepted you. Now, try to take us to Wilderhampton."

"All right." I sling an arm around her waist, holding her firmly to my body, and wish for us to be transported to her home. "It didn't work."

"Maybe we need to do it together. Let's both hold the medallion and try again."

I open my palm. She settles hers onto it, threading her fingers with mine. I assume Charlotte is wishing for us to be transported to her home, and I'm doing the same. But I have my doubts about whether this method will work.

Everything goes black. I can't hear any sounds either.

A flash of light blinds me.

"Open your eyes, love," Charlotte says. "See for yourself."

"Do I have my eyes shut? I can't tell."

She moves my hand onto a soft, pliant lump. "If you don't open your eyes, pet, you won't get to see this."

I peel my lids apart—and smirk. "Maybe I should close my eyes again, so you'll let me fondle you more. How was that supposed to make me open my eyes?"

Charlotte claims my hand. "I needed to do something to wake you up."

"Where are we?"

"At Wilderhampton, of course."

I finally take a moment to examine my surroundings. A large house resides within a larger clearing, and I see at least three floors along with steps that lead up to the front door. A vehicle sits in the driveway, though I don't see anyone inside it.

Charlotte seizes my hand, towing me up the steps to the front door. "We're here, Zane. Isn't this exciting?"

I will reserve my judgment until after I learn how her parents will react to my presence. They should club me to death. I don't expect them to do that, though. If Charlotte is any measure of her family, Kylie and Nathaniel will be courteous. I doubt I'll be greeted with open arms, however. Their courtesy will be tempered and perhaps cool.

Charlotte throws the door open and tows me down a hallway that has high ceilings. All the rooms have their doors closed. Charlotte halts halfway down the hall and hollers, "We're home! Come on out, Mum! You too, Dad! It's time to meet my boyfriend."

I am not a boy, not even by human standards. I look like an adult.

Footfalls clap on the shiny floor, though I can't see anyone yet. Then two figures emerge from one of the rooms. Kylie and Nathaniel Fortescue rush toward us, but they halt a few arm's lengths away.

Nathaniel eyes me with a great deal of skepticism.

His wife seems less skeptical and more confused than anything else.

The former werewolf sheriff of the Outlands rakes his gaze over me, folding his arms over his chest. "Are we meant to celebrate the fact that our daughter has been shagging a demon?"

Kylie nudges him in the side. "Don't be rude, Nathaniel. If Charlotte loves him, he can't be all bad."

"Zane isn't bad at all," Charlotte announces. "He's a wonderful man. And he's also no longer a demon."

Her parents gape at her.

She sets her hands on her hips. "What's wrong with you two? He doesn't even have red skin anymore, but you act like Zane is a horrifying beast. "

Kylie shakes her head slowly. "That's not what had us speechless, sweetie."

"Then what is it?"

"You're in love with him, aren't you? Really, truly, one hundred percent in love with him."

Charlotte gazes up at me with a look of pure adoration. "Yes, I am in love with Zane."

Nathaniel refuses to give up his skepticism, and I don't blame him for that. What was done to him by his own family and my father would scar anyone. But instead of assaulting me, Nathaniel sighs. "I trust Charlotte, and I can tell she hasn't been bewitched. I won't lie to you, though. It will take a very long time for me to accept that a former demon has claimed my daughter's heart. She is our only child, after all, and she means everything to us."

"Charlotte means everything to me as well. She saved my soul."

Kylie rushes up to me and...hugs me. She kisses my cheek too. "Welcome to the family, Zane. Is that your original demon name? Your father had a longer moniker."

"I used to be Zaen'imuth, but now I've rechristened myself Zane. I changed the spelling from Z-A-E-N to Z-A-N-E to sound more human." I did that as part of my plot to seduce their daughter and make her my wanton slave, but I won't confess that detail.

Nathaniel clears his throat, then smiles tightly and slaps my arm. "Might as well go into the drawing room to discuss things. You will be a member of the family soon, and I doubt you understand what that means in the human world."

"I know I have much to learn."

And for the next hour, Nathaniel and Kylie explain the most immediate problems I'll face as a newly minted mortal. Charlotte seems content to sit beside me on the sofa and hold my hand, letting her parents tutor me. I can't learn everything in one day, though.

"Duh," Kylie says. "We had no intention of trying to cram a lifetime of knowledge and experience into your brain in one hour. That sounds impossible, anyway."

"It is possible," I blurt out.

Nathaniel lifts his brows. "You say that as if you know it for certain."

Yes, I've shoved my foot in my mouth yet again. Might as well have it surgically attached to my lips.

Charlotte eyes me with a curious expression. "What are you talking about, Zane?"

I wince and avoid looking at Charlotte or her parents. "I, ah, convinced a demon sorceress to cast a spell to grant me the knowledge of a mortal lifetime in only a moment. I didn't want to attract attention by saying the wrong things or behaving strangely."

"That makes sense," Kylie says. "You didn't want Charlotte to think you were weird or alien."

"Zane is not an alien," Charlotte announces. "Even when he was a demon, he didn't behave like the others. Rahn'omith was a prat who deserved to be incinerated."

Kylie smiles and winks at her daughter. "We get it, sweetie. Zane is your fated mate, just like Nathaniel is mine. You and I are meant to be with these two cavemen."

Charlotte laughs. "Well, we have both visited the Kevitash cave. I guess that makes Dad and Zane cavemen."

I wrap an arm around Charlotte. "That would make you and your mother cavewomen."

No one objects to my statement. In fact, they seem amused by it. Maybe that means they've accepted me and won't demand that I must give up Charlotte and be destroyed as my father had been. But I was never as evil as he was.

That thought stops me. I stare at nothing, not blinking, while a realization rushes through me. Every hair on my body tingles and stands up. I am not evil at all. Perhaps I never was truly a villain. Why else would a good woman like Charlotte fall for me? At last, I have accepted the truth about myself, and it feels incredible.

I burst out laughing.

Kylie and Nathaniel both aim wide-eyed looks at me.

Charlotte seems mildly surprised and even laughs.

I hug her to me and kiss her cheek again and again, all while still laughing. When I crush my mouth to hers for a brief, hard kiss, she grins again even more than she had earlier. Finally, I calm down. But I can't pull away from Charlotte. The warmth of her soft, feminine body feels like heaven.

The woman I love shakes her head. "What in the world brought that on, Zane? I've never seen anyone break into a fit of wild laughter like that."

"I had an epiphany. Isn't that what mortals call it? I suddenly realized that I am not evil and I'm just like all of you now."

Nathaniel rises and approaches me, holding out his hand. "Yes, you are one of us. Welcome to the family, Zane."

We shake hands. And just like that, my new life has begun.

In the weeks that follow, Charlotte and I move into her bedroom suite at Wilderhampton, and I participate in redecorating the room. Charlotte had insisted that we must change the decor to include both our "styles," a term she needs to explain to me since demons don't worry about decor. The furniture in the underworld is strictly utilitarian. Now every night I sleep in a plush bed with Charlotte's warm, supply body cradling mine.

I could live this way forever. But I won't live forever anymore. As a mortal, I could fall prey to any number of diseases and illnesses. That should give me pause, but I've adopted a new attitude about such things. Charlotte calls it "c'est la vie." It's a phrase from a language known as French, and the words mean "that's life."

This is my life now, and I would never trade it for immortality.

One day, the four of us are reclining in chairs on the lawn, enjoying a partly cloudy afternoon. There's a thirty-percent chance of showers, but so far, I haven't seen any evidence of that. With a wind of approximately fifteen miles per hour, the conditions feel perfect to me. Charlotte, Kylie, and Nathaniel smile every time I discuss the weather forecast.

"Give him time," Kylie says. "He'll probably get over his weather obsession after a while. It's all new to him right now."

"Thank you, Kylie, for not laughing at me."

She leans over to pat my arm. "You should get used to calling me Mum or Mom, whichever you prefer. Mum is the British version."

"But Charlotte and I aren't married."

Nathaniel aims a sarcastic glare at me. "How long do plan on living in sin with my daughter?"

"Not as long as you you lived in sin with Kylie. Wasn't it more than a year?"

"You can't count the year when I was in the past and she was in the present."

Nathaniel's mention of living in sin reminds me of something I've been meaning to do. I needed to learn how to drive a car first, so I could visit a shop and buy a particular item. I told Charlotte and her parents that my first solo driving expedition took a few hours because I got lost. I knew precisely where I was going, but this needed to be a secret.

The time has come to reveal the truth.

I get up and offer Charlotte my hand. "Let's go for a walk."

She accepts my hand without hesitation. I help her out of the chair, and we amble across the lawn, heading around the corner of the house to the garden. Only once we're sitting on a concrete bench surrounded by flowering bushes and tall hedges do I enact my plan.

I slide off the bench and drop to one knee.

Her eyes flare wide, though only for a second. Then she bites her lip.

I clasp her left hand. "Charlotte Fortescue, daughter of the wolf, will you spend the rest of your life with me? As my wife?"

She starts to cry. "Yes, you fool, of course I will. I was wondering how long it would take you to ask." She grasps my face and kisses me. "There's nothing I want more than to marry you, Zane."

"And...have children?"

Her smile makes my heart swell, almost as if it might burst. "I can't wait to have little Zanes running around at Wilderhampton."

"Little Charlottes too."

"Dozens of both."

I thrust the ring onto her finger, swoop her up in my arms, and spin us both round and round until I'm dizzy and she must be too. When I set her on her feet, our lips collide, our tongues dance, and the rest of the world fades away. Shrieking and pounding noises erupt from somewhere, but I can't focus on that. Only when we finally stop kissing do I realize what those noises signify.

Kylie has just sprinted into the garden. Nathaniel catches up to her a moment later. They both glance at Charlotte's left hand. Kylie shrieks again, and her husband laughs heartily.

I keep one arm around my fiancée as we turn toward her parents. "If you're done screeching, we have news."

"Yes, yes!" Kylie shouts while hopping on her toes and clapping. "We already figured that out. You two are getting married."

A thunderclap detonates overhead, and the sky turns black.

CHAPTER TWENTY

Charlotte

I TIP MY HEAD BACK TO STUDY THE EVER-DARKENING CLOUDS THAT SEEM to roil with supernatural energies. I swear I can feel the magics nipping at my skin and smell them in the air. Doesn't it just figure that on the day I get engaged, some otherworldly arse would crash the party? I think Zane and I might be cursed after all.

Zane throws an arm around me, pulling me firmly against his side.

Dad has done the same thing with Mum, shielding her with his body. He raises a hand like a visor to squint at the seething sky. Flashes of white ignite in the roiling mass of whatever that is up there.

A bolt of lightning slams down on the lawn not more than thirty feet away. We're all thrown backward, tumbling over on our arses.

But there was no thunderclap this time. A sure sign of mystical forces at work.

Zane flings his arms around me and leaps up, taking me with him. Just as we land on our feet, Mum and Dad scramble to get upright again. My vision is still blinded by that lightning bolt. By the time my vision has recovered reasonably well, I blink swiftly to sort out what I'm seeing.

A figure stands before us.

"Kezia?" I call out. "Is that you?"

The Rom witch ambles closer. "Yes, Charlotte, it's me."

"Why did you put on such a dramatic display? You could've knocked on the front door."

The blackness in the sky has begun to dissipate, and the ringing in my ears is diminishing too.

Kezia smiles. "I enjoy a good show. Don't you?"

Zane squints at her. "You haven't told us why you're here."

"I've come to present an offer."

Mum and Dad have moved up alongside me and Zane. My father eyes Kezia with suspicion. "You were responsible for my daughter being thrown into the Outlands. Why should we trust you now?"

"Because my actions achieved the appropriate result." She waves toward me and Zane. "These two found their fated love, and the multiverse is better for it, just as your love for Kylie improved the state of the Outlands."

Dad squints at her even harder. "How can you believe the Devil's Outlands fared well after Kylie and I left?"

Kezia shakes her head. "You have no idea how long it took me to reconstruct the Outlands in preparation for Zane and Charlotte's arrival. We, the Rom and the Kevitash, combined our magics to resurrect the town. We waited patiently for events to unfold as they must while we kept watch over the four of you. The Kevitash are gone, and the Rom of my tribe were eradicated as well, eventually. But our spirits will never die."

I glance up at Zane, who seems as confused as I am. Then I face Kezia. "Are you dead? Are the people in the Outlands also dead?"

"The answer to both questions is yes and no. The supernatural exists in a gray area between life and death, between apocalypse and eternity."

"Could we skip the riddles? I've never been good at that rubbish."

The Rom witch swings her gaze from me to Mum and Dad, and finally, to Zane. Her sharp gaze is nailed to him. "Everything you endured in your lifetime as a demon prepared you for the opportunity we are giving you. If you accept our offer, your life will change drastically. But we believe you are the only one who might be able to handle the job."

Zane scowls at her. "What job? Speak plainly, or I will toss you into the next county."

Kezia's lips twitch, almost forming a smile. "We want you to become the new sheriff of the Devil's Outlands."

My jaw drops. Zane simply stands beside me like a statue.

After a moment, his brows furrow, and he draws his head back. "You must be insane. The Outlands is a vile domain populated by vile individuals."

The witch lifts her brows. "You were there recently. Did it seem as vile and evil as it once was? Or did the presence of you and Charlotte transform the Outlands?"

Zane hesitates, and I can almost hear the gears turning in his mind. When he speaks again, his tone is cautious. "What is it that you want from me? The position of sheriff is a dangerous full-time job. Charlotte and I live in the normal world, here at Wilderhampton, and we plan to marry and have children. None of that would be possible in the Outlands."

"Why do you assume the position will be full-time?"

This must be the world's strangest job interview. I doubt anyone else has ever been approached by a Rom witch who offered them this kind of deal. But we still haven't heard all the details yet.

I glance up at Zane, and he gives me a tight smile.

"This is a one-time offer," Kezia tells us. "And it expires in twenty-four hours. Before you decide, let me take you to the Outlands, where you can see what the place has become since you left."

Zane looks at me. "I will only go there if you come with me."

"Of course I'll go with you."

"No!" my father shouts. "You will not drag my daughter into the Outlands."

Kezia raises a hand. "Don't worry. You may all come with me."

"That is hardly comforting."

Mum grasps Dad's hand. "I think we should trust Kezia. The Rom and the Kevitash have always helped us."

"Dragging you into the past, into that wretched town, was not helpful at all."

"Yes, it was. We would never have met otherwise. I know you're glad we did, and I know you trust the Rom. You went back in time to get their help in setting up our new life together."

Dad's expression softens as he gazes into Mum's eyes. His lips curl into a sweet smile, and he brushes his fingers over her cheek. "How can I argue with that logic? I've always said I will go anywhere with you, my love."

I grin. "We're all going, then?"

"Yes, pet. I wish you weren't quite so excited by the prospect."

"Let's go there and see what it's like now, before you pronounce it to be a wicked place."

"As you wish."

Kezia waves her arms toward the sky and tilts her head back, chanting in another language.

The world spins around us. Zane clutches me to his body just as I clutch him. I can't see anything, but I feel supernatural energies whirling wildly, propelling us higher and higher until we reach the pinnacle of whatever this is.

And then we free-fall.

Every one of us, even the blokes, let out panicked cries as we tumble downward faster and faster. I squeeze my eyes shut and cling to Zane, fully expecting to go splat on the ground. We'll be a puddle flesh.

Our free-fall ends.

The silence deafens me, but it doesn't seem like I've been crushed into a puddle. I feel the warmth and firmness of Zane's body still holding on to me. My feet seem to have touched down on a surface. The ground? Can't figure what else it might be.

"Charlotte, open your eyes."

Zane's voice pulls me out of my confusion. I peel my lids open. His sweet expression melts me from the inside out, and I sag against him. "We're alive. Aren't we?"

"Yes, baby. Look around."

I turn my head this way and that, my surprise growing with every second that elapses. "We're in the Outlands. But it looks...different."

"Somewhat, yes. Maybe we should let Kezia explain."

Mum and Dad are standing beside us, but the Rom witch faces all of us while standing a short distance away.

Kezia spreads her arms in the sort of grand gesture she seems to enjoy. "This is the new and improved version of the Outlands. The town itself has been upgraded, as mortals might say. The dregs of the world are still sent here as punishment for their depraved acts. However, now this has become a place for redemption."

"Redemption?" Dad says. "The inhabitants have always been irredeemable."

"We have changed the rules. The Outlands is no longer an enclave run by demons. Henceforth, it will offer everyone a second chance which they may accept or refuse. But refusal means damnation."

Zane takes a step toward Kezia. "Damnation means destruction. You want me to mete out capital punishment, but I have no taste for death anymore."

"We're glad to hear that. Self-defense is the only sort of death we would want you to mete out."

"You expect me to police this town. That is indeed a full-time job, and I don't want to live here."

I move to stand beside him. "Let her finish, Zane. I don't think she intends for you to police the town twenty-four seven."

"That is correct, Charlotte," Kezia says. "Zane will not need to be present all the time or even most of the time. He has retained just enough magics to let him keep an eye on things from afar."

"Are you saying we could have normal lives? I can still work at my school, and Zane can take on a regular job too."

Zane scrunches his brows. "Is that what you mean, Kezia?"

She smiles. "Yes. And if you accept our offer, we will employ all our magics to provide a foolproof history for you, Zane, so that you will have no trouble finding a vocation, buying property, whatever you need."

Goodness gracious, I can't believe what Kezia and her kin are offering us. The Rom had provided similar assistance for my father after Zor'imuth was destroyed. Dad was born and raised in the Victorian era, after all. But the

Daughters of Erosabel had created an impeccable fake history for him as well as ensuring he and Mum would have a comfortable lifestyle.

Now Zane and I could have the same benefits, thanks to my ancestors.

"There is one other issue," Kezia says. "We are aware of what the demon sorceress did for you, Zane, but she failed to explain that the spell would gradually draw the life out of your body until you die. That was the toll she mentioned. We have neutralized it."

"I appreciate that. And I'm not surprised that Mazdala lied. But why did you harass me and try to kill me?"

"Did I murder you? No. You are so obstinate that we needed a stronger inducement to convince you to choose the right path. I pushed you only as far as necessary."

"I can't deny I would have ignored a gentle suggestion or even the crack of a mace on my skull." My fiancé cants his head left and right while his brows crinkle. His gaze remains fixated on the Rom witch. «I›m confused, Kezia. How can you come and go like a ghost when you are alive."

She glances at me. "Your demon is much smarter than we expected." Kezia turns back to Zane. "I am not like a ghost. I *am* a ghost. My mortal body died long, long ago while my spirit lived on. The Daughters of Erosabel have kept my secret ever since the day I cursed Zor'imuth. That spell drained me, and I should have died, but my sister witches cast another spell that kept me alive until all my children had reached adulthood. I believe you understand now."

Zane pulls me close, though he faces the Rom witch. "You are a ghost because you are Erosabel."

"What?" I all but shout, whirling my head around to stare at Zane. "How did you know that? No one ever told me, and Mum never knew."

Erosabel approaches us, now only inches away from us. "I can at times assume a mortal form, but I must always return to the realm in which my departed daughters reside in what most people would call heaven."

"You deceived us. I believed you were Kezia, a Rom witch."

My ancestor folds her hands around mine. "Please forgive me, Charlotte. This was the only way to ensure the desired outcome. You and Zane are the most obstinate couple, and it required a great deal of magics to nudge you two in the right direction. Zaen'imuth never fit into the demon world because he is not an evil, sadistic monster. He's a good man who once hid behind a demon facade."

Zane shakes his head slowly. "But I committed horrible acts."

"Not once have you murdered an innocent. Only in self-defense or in battle have you ever taken a life." Erosabel lays a hand on his cheek. "No one but you could give Charlotte what she deserves—eternal devotion, the kind that persists beyond the grave. And she gives you the same. Your souls have always been mated."

Erosabel kisses his cheek, then mine. "Now, I must return to the other realm. I and my daughters will always watch over you. And know that everything unfolded as it was meant to. If ever you should need us again, we will come to you. Blessed be, my children."

The Daughters of Erosabel vanish. Erosabel herself lingers momentarily, then disappears—with a radiant smile on her face.

A few days later, Zane mysteriously acquires all the paperwork and background information he needs to become an average mortal. The Daughters of Erosabel made sure of that. Zane even has a genealogy chart that lists his fictional forebears. My soon-to-be husband also acquired a sizable bank account. I will continue working at the school, but Zane has decided to go to university and earn a degree in psychology so he can help confused people who have nasty relatives. Zane is certainly qualified for the job. He has personal experience.

I have no doubts he will excel and become a fantastic therapist.

Our wedding is a small affair that takes place on the lawn at Wilderhampton. Erosabel returns to observe the festivities, and my three best mates get to meet her. They don't know Erosabel is a witch or that she's, um, no longer living. Eden, Darcy, and Amelia adore Zane. Well, why shouldn't they? He is the sexiest creature in any realm, and he's become quite adept at small talk.

Jenna and Megan, mum's two best mates, fly in for the ceremony too.

And five months after the wedding, Zane and I receive wonderful news. We're going to have a baby. Despite everything we both went through, Zane and I found our fairy-tale ending.

Did you love

Visit

AnnaDurand.com

to subscribe to her newsletter
for updates on forthcoming books
&
to receive exclusive content!

ANNA DURAND IS A BESTSELLING, MULTI-AWARD-WINNING AUTHOR OF contemporary and paranormal romance. Her books have earned bestseller status on every major retailer and wonderful reviews from readers around the world. But that's the boring spiel. Here are some really cool things you want to know about Anna!

Born on Lackland Air Force Base in Texas, Anna grew up moving here, there, and everywhere thanks to her dad's job as an instructor pilot. She's lived in Texas (twice), Mississippi, California (twice), Michigan (twice), and Alaska—and now Ohio.

As for her writing, Anna has always invented stories in her head, but she didn't write them down until her teen years. Those first awful books went into the trash can a few years later, though she learned a lot from those stories. Eventually, she would pen her first romance novel, the paranormal romance Willpower, and she's never looked back since.

To get exclusive content, join Anna's Facebook group, Anna's Romance Addicts, or sign up for her newsletter.

www.ingramcontent.com/pod-product-compliance
Lightning Source LLC
Chambersburg PA
CBHW071931190726
48293CB00004B/1239